Anonymous

A Tourist Idyl and Other Stories

Vol. 2

Anonymous

A Tourist Idyl and Other Stories
Vol. 2

ISBN/EAN: 9783337328740

Printed in Europe, USA, Canada, Australia, Japan

Cover: Foto ©Andreas Hilbeck / pixelio.de

More available books at **www.hansebooks.com**

AND OTHER STORIES.

IN TWO VOLUMES.

VOL. II.

LONDON:

SAMPSON LOW, MARSTON, SEARLE & RIVINGTON,

CROWN BUILDINGS, 188, FLEET STREET.

1883.

LONDON:
PRINTED BY WILLIAM CLOWES AND SONS, LIMITED,
STAMFORD STREET AND CHARING CROSS.

CONTENTS OF VOL. II.

—◆◇◆—

THREE FRAGMENTS OF AUTOBIOGRAPHY

(*Continued*).

BICE.

My mother's sister, Beatrice, was one of the
host of women that have been named after
Dante's spirit-love—about the only one, in my
judgment, that ever really merited such a dis-
tinction. It has been my peculiar, and in some
respects rather painful, experience to be bored
by women. Apart from the dressing, painting
idiot who has forfeited her claim to be considered of the same species as Griselda, or
Portia, or Sophia, I find them, as a rule, either
exceedingly superficial or insufferably stupid.
Bice is the exception, and if I were a Dante,
instead of being obscure Lancelot Golding, with
exactly brains enough for a clerkship in a
Government Office, and the accumulation of a
small library of editorial regrets and thanks, I
should have sung her my Divine Comedy long

ago. Well! I'll do what I can for her in that line. Many's the time, when we lived down at Altham, that I told her I would, just to pacify her after a long tirade on the inferiority of her sex. I was nothing but a bumptuous schoolboy then, and richly deserved the "jaws" I got for presuming to have an opinion at all on the subject, though I will say for myself that I invariably wound up with the logical anti-climax, that there was no creature in human shape more beautiful, virtuous, and personally satisfactory to me than Bice herself.

We understood each other. There was a peculiar tie between us, owing to our having been brought up together, and to her being just near enough to me in age to share all my youthful vagaries, and just enough ahead of me to keep a motherly look-out when they threatened to grow serious. My parents died before I can remember, and I went at once to live with my grandmother and the uncle and aunt who were so much more my own contemporaries than my mother's that they have always been to me simply Edgar and Bice. What good times we used to have down there! We weren't rich. My grandmother had nothing but a small jointure and a little house she bought in the early days of her widowhood, when she couldn't bring herself to leave the old place, though she knew very well into what sort of hands the estate had fallen. That was the one thing that would have made one wish to leave Altham—the proximity to a scamp like Jim Blake Johnstone; but the grandmother always had a kind of lurking fondness for her step-son, and then he was so much away that we of Altham Cottage nearly always had the run of the Hall and the grounds—except in the shooting season. But what I shall never forget, what we all of us shall never forget, is the first autumn that Jim was obliged to let the Hall. I suppose his affairs were in a worse mess than usual, or he found the county getting a bit hot for him, or he had attractions elsewhere—anyhow, let the old place was, for the first time on record, and great was the stir in the village occasioned by the event. I was just home from the Continent, where I had been living two or three years, and was coquetting with various " careers," two of which have always had strong attractions for irresolute sciolism, and had for me—literature and painting. I had the amiable belief of two-and-twenty in my own capacity to excel in either, but Edgar, himself a literary man, chaffed me out of the one, and Bice, who drew like an angel, teased me out of the other,

and it ended in my accepting a proffered nomination from a relative in high places for the
Office which has since had the honour of indoc-
trinating me with laziness and red-tapeism.

I was in a *désœuvré*, holiday mood at the time
—just the sort of mood in which fellows fall in
love who haven't (without conceit be it spoken)
such an exalted conception of the ideal woman
as not to discover anything particular to fall in
love with in the average real one ; and I used
to think, as I mooned about the place, watching the preparations for the advent of the
strangers, what a romance some people would
have begun to weave about them already.
There was just the right sort of novelish
atmosphere of mystery about the Delormes.
Jim had probably never been at the pains to
let his step-mother know who her new neighbours were to be, though it did occur to him
to say in the one letter she got, dated from
Spa, " My last will have told you all I know of
Delorme." In another part of the same letter,
he wrote, " Mind you're civil to the Delormes.
I was obliged to let you in for it talking over
things here, and he knows I've written about it.
He's quite your sort," Jim had the grace to add,
by which we three, Edgar, Bice, and I, understood a covert sneer at respectable, church-going,

debt-paying, good breeding; and wondered what accident had brought such a man and Jim Blake Johnstone together. That was about all the information we had concerning the new-comers, when my grandmother, who was be-coming more and more of an invalid, and seldom went out herself, despatched us to leave her cards on them. How well I remember that afternoon! How I hated going out in the August heat, though the walk was only under the trees in the park, those glorious old elms that I always have loved, and always shall love, as though they were my own. I was busy over a picture which I was getting ready for Bice's birthday—(her twenty-ninth, I don't mind say-ing, because, though it does sound prosaic, nothing but poetry ever was, or ever could be, associated with Bice)—and, logically, I was very cross with *her* for dragging me out to pay morning calls. Edgar enjoyed complete immu-nity from such liabilities. Nobody would have dreamed of dragging *him* from the seclusion of the den where he performed his scientific experiments, and wrote anthropologic papers for the magazines, to make him array himself in civilized attire and go and jabber nothings with people who didn't know Tyndall from Burne Jones.

"I can't think why you can't leave me alone as you do Edgar," I observed sulkily to Bice on this occasion.

She responded with the look she always gave me when I grumbled, a comical, half-reproachful, half-incredulous, expression that set us both laughing. Then, without further comment, she took me by the arm and set off with that peculiar jerky step unknown to *premières danseuses*, but much affected by rollicking village maids, three in a row, on their way home from school. Not a child in Altham that looked sweeter and rosier than Bice, for all the twenty-nine Augusts that had passed over her smooth forehead. She had had no wear and tear, none, I mean, of the external, physical sort; and if her spirits ever flagged, if from one cause or another she ever was anything but the chattering, mirthful, mercurial sunbeam and solace of the house, all I can say is, we never knew it. She looked so delicious that afternoon, in her big hat and summer drapery, that I couldn't help telling her so, obliquely.

"I hope there are no young Delormes, for their own sakes, Bice."

"Indeed, I hope there are no young *Miss* Delormes," said wicked Bice, with a mock sigh, "considering that you are the only beau in the neighbourhood, eligible or ineligible. Poor things! less promising material for a flirtation it would be impossible to imagine. When are you going to be like other boys, Lance?"

"When you're like other girls, Bice. I mean, when other women are like you—instead of being either fools or bores. These Miss Delormes, for instance, in my mind's eye I see them. Tall, sparkling, curved, with a veneer of foreign mannerism added to the proclivities of the fast young Englishwoman. Fond of gambling, faugh! scoffers at Ruskin and Carlyle. Or, if you like it better, homely featured and impassive, addicted to needlework and stories for the young. Good heavens! They've seen the Mediterranean in summer without going mad, and they confuse the Madonna della Seggiola with the Madonna di San Sisto!"

"There, that'll do, they'll hear you," commented Bice, as she pulled me up the steps.

We asked for Mrs. Delorme as a matter of course, and were a little taken aback when the servant, a shrewd-looking Frenchman with the genial plasticity of countenance characteristic of the foreign flunkey, smilingly informed us that *Miss* Delorme was in the garden. He led us through the house (as if we wanted leading through that house!) and out on to the broad expanse of smooth-shaven lawn at the back, where, some distance off, under the shade of the lofty trees that bordered it nearly the whole way round, we espied a little group of people. They were dwarfed by the tall trees and the distance, and yet we were surprised to find not more than two when we got up to them—a lady lying on a couch covered with soft white drapery, and a girl standing by her with a big fan which she was plying with scrupulous carefulness and incomparable grace. When she became conscious of our approach, she turned round swiftly, closed the fan with a sweep of the hand, and advanced a pace or two, fixing upon us those large black round delicious eyes which from that moment forth have made my only heaven.

Oh, she was beautiful to the man, beautiful to the poet, thrice beautiful to the artist! She was so young, I thought her a child at first, but she had about her what one thirsts for here in frigid, neutral England—the warmth and glow and glamour of the South; small, but kindling with energy and emotion; dark-skinned, ripe, like the children of the South; in form faultless, in feature not so irreproachable perhaps, but to me sufficient, and worshipful beyond my wildest dreams. Before she said a word to me she had enslaved me. Like one of the most admirable and least admired of George Sand's heroines, " she took my heart from me, as though she had drawn it from my bosom with her two hands, and carried it away, probably without attaching more importance to it than to a leaf plucked idly in passing from a bough by the roadside."

I held back a little, gazing, while the Frenchman announced " Miss Blake Johnstone," and Bice extended her hand to the dark-eyed apparition. Dear Bice, she was blushing a little, from shyness. She could not tell what sort of associations these people might have with the name of Blake Johnstone, and I don't know what vague terrors shot through her when the gipsy rejected her hand and gave her a stately bow, at the same time making way for her to pass to the lady on the sofa. The invalid, then, taking such marked precedence of her younger companion, must be Miss Delorme ? She was a woman of fifty or thereabouts, of refined and regular features, and a fine transparency of skin, denoting not so much illness as native delicacy of texture ; and when she smiled I thought her face one of the sweetest I ever saw. She greeted us both kindly, and begged us to sit down. " I think there are chairs, Gyp?" she added, turning her head half round, with an effort, to see.

Still that fierce, defiant attitude on the part of Gyp. She scarcely responded, but went on standing at her post by the couch, with erect head, and eyes still darting suspicion, now at Bice, now at me. Presently she took up some yellow roses from the table and fastened her eyes upon them, while she passed them from one brown hand to the other. Miss Delorme and Bice were chatting. It seemed my part to address her.

"You are staying here? I have not seen you in church."

"We do not go to your church. We are Catholics. We go to the Catholic Chapel at Queen's Stepping."

"Ah, I go there sometimes. I am sorry you don't come to our church, though. Will you not——"

"*Never*," interrupted the gipsy, before she knew what I was going to say.

"Please don't snub me like that!"

"What is 'snub'?" abruptly. The question was explained by her foreign accent, her Italian accent, as I determined it to be. She was Italian too in her matter-of-factness. For is not Dante himself matter-of-fact in his grand, imaginative way?

"'Snub' is to be stern and fierce to a poor artist, who has seen no Madonnas since he left the shores of Italy," I said deprecatingly, finishing with a laugh, as one talks to a beautiful child. "And the way one atones for it is this. One gives him a yellow rose to paint, the most shapely and the most richly scented of all."

My foolish young head was on fire. Heaven knows what sweet delirious thoughts I had, and what nonsense I talked.

"*You* know Italy? *You* have painted in Italy?" she cried, disregarding the nonsense. A light spread over the eager face that was radiant enough before; the features relaxed, and instead of reticence and suspicion there was the frankest ingenuous enthusiasm. "Ah, I paint too. You will help me with my drawings, will you not?"

She was sitting beside me now, close beside me on a low seat; but the next instant she was on her feet again.

"Come *now!* *Zia*, may I take Mr. Golding into the house to tell me what to do to the eyes of my *contadina?*"

I wonder if the *Zia* ever refused such a request in her life? She paused a moment, though, glancing critically in my direction. I endeavoured to look as harmless as possible,

and as absolutely unconcerned as though the
prospect of a few minutes alone with my en-
chantress were not—well, what such a prospect
is to a man whose first and last and only love is
dawning rapidly upon him. Probably my
youthful and unsophisticated air reassured her ;
and, indeed, a far more penetrating duenna
might have been baffled by my babyish light
curls, blue eyes, and *dégagé*, undangerous get-
up. I had not changed a well-worn shooting-
coat, to spite Bice for teasing me to go ; I wore
knickerbockers that day ; my old straw hat had
a bit of pale-coloured ribbon round it. The
result was an amiable boy of eighteen.

"Yes, dear," said Miss Delorme, bestowing
another of her nice smiles on me. "And Gyp,
dear, see if you can find your father."

Gyp nodded her head, and set off towards
the house with a deliberate stateliness of step
which struck me as un-English—unnatural, at
all events, in English girls as enthusiastic as
herself. She was at no pains to find her father
till she had accomplished her object and taken me
into the morning-room to show me the little
watercolour drawing which was clearly absorbing
her whole mind. It was a sketch from life of
an Italian peasant-woman—crude enough, but
bearing abundant marks of nascent talent, of
the high order which is born of love.

"Ah, we had to go before I could finish it," she said, lifting up her great eyes to me with a look that was absolutely piteous, "and it refuses to be finished here in England. I cannot get the colouring. I cannot make it come right."

"Let us see whether it is so impossible," I said, taking the thing from her, and wrestling with a vehement inclination to stoop and kiss "the eyes of her *contadina*" that were so like her own, for all their defective shading and singular expression that declined to come right. I am glad to say I did vanquish it, and merely looked at them wisely. Speak? Oh, how could I speak to her about them; tell her her blunder, point out this omission, and suggest that alteration, when she was gazing up at me so wistfully, hanging on my lips with mingled impatience and humility? So I only said, "Your *contadina* is very beautiful. May I take her home with me, and try to finish her for you?"

She gave a short sigh of relief. "It is very good of you. Yes; please take it home. I know I could *never* do it myself, yet I want it done."

"It shall be done," I said; "only, you know, artists do not paint for nothing."

She looked puzzled for a moment. "Ah, the rose!" she cried, laughing. Then, with a little coquettish toss of the head, "We left those behind. But there are more. You shall come into the rose-garden, and have as many as I can find for you."

"Certainly, you owe me the rose, but I want something more if I finish your picture."

"You are greedy. What is it?"

"That I may be allowed to paint you."

"Ah, when you like. I have sat to artists in Rome, often," Gyp said, in a provokingly matter-of-course way, as she sauntered out of doors again, and through shady, winding paths, to the fine old kitchen garden where, I knew better than she, the roses grew. They clustered round a fish-pond in the centre, and you reached them by four grassy walks, bordered with hazels. The gooseberry bushes were quite shut out—if that is a satisfaction to anybody. For my own part, I should have preferred to see them, and the loaded espaliers, and the dear old guardian walls, twelve feet high and more, covered to the topmost brick with giant plums, and figs, and apricots, and peaches. The Altham kitchen garden was renowned throughout the county, and I had spent my happiest boyish days there, reading Walter Scott and Dickens in the shade, and munching all the fruit I could lay hands on. But I leave you to imagine if I had ever thought it a hundredth part so glorious as on this August afternoon, when I strolled through it with Gyp Delorme, whose every movement had more poetry in it than a library of Scott, and whose face was a bit of living Southern sunshine. She was lingering over a rose-tree, seeking out the blooms that the summer heat had harmed the least, when she suddenly looked up at me.

" You are not like Mr. Blake Johnstone," she said quickly, adding reflectively, " your name is Golding."

" Yes; he is only my half-uncle," I rejoined hastily. " You did not like him ? "

" I like no one who is without religion," Gyp said, very earnestly, ceasing to gather the roses, and stepping back into the shade of the hazels.

She stood there with her hands crossed, the flowers drooping from them, the background of green boughs throwing out her dark, uplifted head. I should have liked to paint her so—in the same spot, the same attitude, the same gown —a sort of buff with crimson bows. But her reality, the intensity of conviction with which she spoke, detached my thoughts from picture-making. From what unheard-of realm of Faëry had this strange being dropped, taking life so simply, yet so solemnly, talking religion with big, serious eyes, instead of simpering common-places, bantering, or flirting?

"*He* was without religion," she continued gravely. "My father says he had other faults. I do not know. We all have faults. But to me, to despise the great good God, to scoff at His church and at His priests, is worse than anything. Is it possible to hate Him? Him— who made me, and gave me my father, and made this pretty, beautiful earth, and made— *Italy?* Oh, one must be bad to hate One so good. I *hate* the people that hate religion!" cried Gyp, with a sudden outburst of Italian vehemence, and a captivating naïve uncon- sciousness of any inconsequence.

"*She* is his sister!"

I had to turn and look in the direction of Gyp's eyes before I found out that the words referred to Bice, whom she had espied in the distance, coming along one of the turf avenues with—I supposed—Mr. Delorme. Whether her unfortunate name alone earned her the angry glance with which the words were accompanied I could not tell, but it was a very angry glance Gyp gave her. Then, turning to me, "Come, I must present you to my father."

For the moment the fire and fervour had vanished. It was now the same frigid courtesy

with which we had been greeted at first. But
no sooner was the ceremony of introduction
over, than Gyp laid hold of one hand of her
father, and placed his arm round her own neck,
resting the hand on her shoulder. The movement was not a caressing one; it was as though
she were taking him under her protection. She
did not smile, even when he chid her playfully.

"Did not the *Zia* send you for me? And I
find you playing truant among the roses!
Lucky for you that I happened to see her and
her visitor on the lawn!"

"Who wouldn't play truant in such a
garden?" smiled Bice. "You don't know how
he and I like being here again."

"Ah, you were going to show me those renowned bee-hives, that I haven't succeeded in
finding," rejoined Mr. Delorme, making as
though he would shake off Gyp and walk on
with Bice. But Gyp clung to his hand, just
looking up once with a dumb appeal, that was
either very childish and absurd, or else meant
more than we could know. He answered her
with a smile, rather deprecating, indeed, but
full of a more exquisite absorbing tenderness
than I ever knew before that fathers felt, and,
the mute dialogue over, they moved forward,

he trying to make it seem as though Bice were walking abreast of them, though there was really not room for this, and she was a little behind them, while I followed alone. I was glad enough to be allowed to follow and watch, and now and then answer a stray question or remark that was addressed to me. To say nothing of Gyp, I was as much struck with Mr. Delorme as I had been with his sister. He was older by a year or two, and his head was getting decidedly grey, but he escaped looking elderly, as men do who cut their hair close, and wear nothing but a moustache, and he had just the same refined clear-cut contour of face and engaging sweetness of expression. What ill-health had done for her in the way of adding a deeper interest to that natural sweetness, I fancied I could detect that trouble had done for him. I began to imagine that that child's mother must have one day been to him all and more than all that that child was now, and that he had lost her. I began to feel a certain curiosity about Gyp's mother, and when we had returned to Miss Delorme, and I was talking to her about the drawing, while the other three were looking for the church spire behind the trees, I said, by way of a leading question, "How can any *Englishwoman* feel so passion-

ately for beauty and art and religion, especially
one so young?"

But Miss Delorme only answered, "You see,
my niece has passed nearly the whole seventeen
years of her life abroad."

"Her mother was an Italian?" I persisted,
with the rashness of youth, naïvely probing,
as young fools do, regions which older people
know better than to pry into.

There was a momentary pause, during which
I felt rather than saw that I had violated some
sanctuary.

Then came the plain monosyllable, "Yes."

"We will come for Gyp's picture when it is
finished," Mr. Delorme said, as he turned to us,
fancying his remark à propos. "I am promised
an introduction to Mr. Edgar Blake Johnstone,
whose writings have interested me more than
once, and Mrs. Blake Johnstone, you say, one
is likely to find——"

"Always, now," said Bice, with a little sigh.

"My sister's enemy, neuralgia, imprisons
her——"

"Oh, a host of troubles! But you will come
and see her?" added Bice, in her most cordial
way, as she extended her hand for good-bye.

II.

I SHALL not forget Bice as we walked home that evening. She was, at times, graver than I ever saw her in my life; at other times she was gayer, full of noisy irrepressible mirth which jarred me, as such spasmodic outbursts do when one wants to be left to one's own ecstatic thoughts. Not a syllable did she say about the Delormes—no chaff, no criticism, no expressions of pleasure. All she said, when she was not wrapped in thought, was mere idle nonsense, humbug about the deer or the rabbits, or the holes in my coat. I had never known her so odd. At dinner, of course, she was obliged to give her mother and Edgar full particulars of the new tenants, and I began to writhe with terror lest she should level some sly side-hit at the defeated Benedict (I was really not in the least like Benedict, only, of course, every one else thought so) opposite her. I am very glad for her own sake she didn't, for I was never less disposed to be chaffed in my whole life. I was in a sort of feverish, highly strung state, only avoiding saying what I had better not by saying nothing, and, had I been stung, I should have been quite capable of throwing my plate at the offender's head. I wouldn't for worlds Edgar knew what made me rush upstairs the moment the ladies withdrew, leaving him sitting there over his wine in the loose cool summer gear he had declined to change, stroking his fair beard, and brooding over the dynamic properties of light. I wanted to put a stroke or two to my *contadina*—her *contadina*—before dark, and I tore Bice's birthday-picture from my easel, enthroned the dark-eyed beauty there, and set to work. Usually I was strolling with Bice in the garden at that hour. I could see her waiting for me as I worked close to the window, loitering by herself, her white gown glinting among the flower-beds. I saw her without seeing her, without thinking of her, without so much as remembering to call her from the window that I was busy and could not come to her. So she presently came to me. Bice never knocked at the door of that room, for it was her sitting-room as well as my studio, and she came in now with as little ceremony as usual, and proceeded, as her manner was, to hook back my two arms in hers, and look over my shoulder at what I was doing.

" Ah, not mine ! " she said quickly.

" Yours shall be finished to-morrow," I said,

disengaging myself from her grasp, and feeling, for the first time, a little conscience-stricken and confused.

Any one that knew what we two had been to each other must have wondered at the calmness with which Bice turned away from me to pick up her drawing from the floor. She took it to the other window and examined it for a long while in silence. At last her voice startled me.

"Lance, I don't want this finished. I want to have it as it is, just as you left it this morning. May I?"

"Bice! Don't be absurd! What do you mean? It isn't like *you* to have fads of this kind!"

I spoke irritably, because I half saw through her.

"Just this once, old boy!" she rejoined gaily. "Just one fad in a lifetime! Oh, Lance, Lance, what's the good of shamming innocent with *me*? Don't you think I know that it's all changed since this morning? Don't you think I see that it's come at last, as I always thought it would come—all in a moment? Why, you goose, did you think that with such a warm heart and lively imagination and silly excitable brain as yours, you would be proof

for the tenth part of an instant against such a
dear little exquisite creature as that? If *you*
did, *I* knew better. I saw in a moment that
she was to be my niece, and made up my mind
to abdicate in her favour as any superannuated
aunt with a sense of duty would."

"Bice, don't talk nonsense. You're not my
aunt, and I don't see that it's a question of
abdication."

"Very well, then it isn't. Just give me a
kiss, and let me know at any time when you're
in want of an aide-de-camp."

And exit Bice laughing, with the light step
characteristic of her.

It had been one of Bice's daily labours of love
to drive her mother out in our little pony-
carriage, until lately, when increasing illness
had made the exertion undesirable. For some
weeks our patient had left the house and garden
but seldom, and when one afternoon, a few days
after our visit to the Hall, she expressed a wish
to go out, we all took the line of dissuading her,
thinking it an invalid's fancy which it might
be imprudent to gratify. I, individually, had
more reasons than one for dissuading her. I
had a presentiment that the Delormes would
return our visit that day, and I did not want
Bice to be out. Suppose Edgar took it into his

head to go out too, they wouldn't come in to see *me*. However, she persisted, with querulous doggedness, and Bice, bracing herself up to rather more cheerfulness than usual, ended by carrying off her wearying charge, a good-hearted soul enough, but having the knack for torturing others of good-hearted souls— people of unquestioned worth, irritable nerves, and what I once heard a clever woman call " a teaspoonful of religion."

" Have a walk, Lance ? "

The question was shouted up to me from the garden by Edgar, as soon as the ladies were gone. I put my head out. There he stood, all ready, pipe in mouth, hat pulled well over his eyes for shade.

" Too hot. Besides, I've got my review to finish."

" Hang your review ! Come out ! "

" Don't be an idiot, Edgar. By-and-by, when it's cooler. Just come up here—can't you ?—and tell me something about the Gnostics."

" Not in my line. Can tell you something about the Veddahs—Hullo ! Wheels ! "

And the misanthropical anthropologist made a dive into his den through the nearest open window.

But he was not to get off so easily this time. He was asked for when it was ascertained that his mother was not at home, and had presently to appear just as he was in the drawing-room. I laughed as I heard his suave tones mingling with the deeper ones of the visitor, who I felt certain was Mr. Delorme. I knew he wasn't above heartily wishing he'd got on respectable clothes. I was profoundly busy over my critique, so busy that I did not even turn my head to answer him when, a few minutes later, old Bush, our dear old man-servant, came hobbling up to inform me that Mr. and Miss Delorme were downstairs. I went on scribbling —on the blotter—not, luckily for my literary reputation, the paper—for some time afterwards. My hand was shaking like a girl's, my head was swimming; I nearly made up my mind I would not go down at all. I was still wavering, when, to my amazement, I heard steps on the stairs, and old Edgar burst the door open with, " Some visitors, Lance."

" We mustn't disturb you," said Mr. Delorme, pausing on the threshold.

" Oh, please come in," I cried, flinging the pen on to the floor, where there were sundry letters, sketches, and books of reference to keep it company.

"We heard you were somewhere on the premises, and I suggested a search, by way of a pretext for seeing as much of this charming house as possible," said Mr. Delorme, making way for Gyp to shake hands with me. What did he do it for? Why did he bring her? Didn't he see that she was enough to dazzle even a cold-blooded scientist like Edgar, in the buff and crimson dress, and large hat with plume of crimson feathers, and quaintly wrought silver ornaments that suited her rich type of beauty and mingled stateliness and simplicity.

"I am glad you should see my room. It is the nicest in the house," I said, talking at random, "especially the creepers. I can pick six different kinds of flowers out of one window."

"And the seat in the window!" exclaimed Gyp, in a kind of grave breathless ecstasy, seating herself as a child does in a new tempting nook, among the crimson cushions where Bice and I indulged in fits of laziness or meditation. There, surrounded by her own colour, with a mullioned casement framed in creepers behind her, in a pose unsurpassable for natural dignity and grace, she made an even lovelier picture than she had done in the Altham rose garden, and I was so enchanted with her that,

as usual, I lost control over myself, and called
out in my idiotic, impetuous way, "Miss
Delorme, you said I might try. and paint you.
How I should like to get you just as you are
now—this moment!"

If Delorme had been anything but the refined
courteous fellow he was, he might have given
me the set-down I deserved for presuming so
far on such a slight acquaintance, but he
seemed to understand exactly how it was, and
not to be displeased with me. He was one of
those rare men that have seen life through and
through, and have all the world has to give,
and yet have never lost their early—what shall
I call it, simplicity or guilelessness of mind? I
don't know that the word for it exists; what I
mean is that the man hadn't a worldly thought,
and that when he saw that his child had
inspired a genuine, honest love, though only in
a harum-scarum boy with no particular pros-
pects, he rather liked it than not.

"Is there any reason the first sketch shouldn't
be made now?" he asked kindly, looking from
Gyp to me, and from me to Gyp. "We are in
no hurry, unless it would be trespassing on
your time?"

Gyp Delorme turned her head a little, to
give me such a look as I had not thought

to win from her, until after months of unrepaid
devotion. It was as though I interested her,
as though she were bestowing her whole mind
and attention in trying to sound me and find
out what I meant by this strange *empressement*,
as though I were worth, actually worth, her
minute and careful study. After she had given
her consent with a half-smile, she resumed the
same unabashed serious gaze, and it was all I
could do to work steadily under it, and not in
despair throw aside the pencil that could never
hope to render half her mysterious charm.

Edgar helped me by taking Mr. Delorme in
hand, and entertaining him in his calm, unconcerned way, as if there were no such volcanic
disturbances going on at his elbow, or anything
in the world of more importance than the recon-
struction of the alphabet. The two had a good
deal in common, and many and various were
the current topics, literary and scientific, they
touched upon, Delorme drawing out Edgar as
very few people could, and Edgar gleaning many
a suggestion and useful hint from him, as clever
men do, even when they are not talking to their
equals in enlightenment. Gyp and I weren't
very much edified by it all, but we didn't
speak, so I heard it all in a way, with much
inward thankfulness at the prospect of a fresh

link being created between the Hall and the Cottage.

After a while my grandmother and Bice came in, and Edgar went down to tell them of our visitors. He was some time gone, and in his absence Mr. Delorme amused himself taking up one book after another from the table, now and then making some comment, to which I did my best to respond coherently.

" Ah, who reads this?" he said once, half inadvertently, I thought.

I looked round. It was a book of Bice's, a theological work by a continental writer, whose name I shall not mention, because he is a *bête noire* to many, and I do not choose to have Bice's name associated with so much as a suspicion of wilful irreverence. I do not go in for that sort of thing myself, but I will answer for any theological book she reads and likes, that it has never done anything but tighten her grasp of truth, and extend and deepen her powers of loving.

" Ah, Miss Blake Johnstone," Delorme said again, when I had told him. He presently became absorbed in the book, holding it up to read as he stood. Suddenly Gyp caught sight of its cover, where the title was emblazoned in good-sized type.

"Do not read that book, father," she exclaimed, in her deep earnest tones. Then, recollecting herself, "Oh, I beg your pardon for moving. There! Is that right?"

"She keeps my *index expurgatorius*," her father said, smiling. I noticed that he put down the volume immediately, but it was only to take up another by an English critic of greater acumen perhaps, but far less devoutness. Gyp saw the title of that too.

"Is that book also your aunt's?" she asked me, this time without moving. The intensity of purpose in her eyes redeemed the question from impertinence. I suspected it of being one of those Bice read and did *not* like, but I was not thinking over much of guarding Bice's interests then, and merely answered "Also" in her own sweet catching idiom. I could not, however, help being struck by the marked increase in stiffness in her manner to Bice, when she joined us a minute or two afterwards, leaving Edgar to help his mother up to her own room. I saw, too, that Bice was a little bit nonplussed by it. Her colour came and went faster than usual, and without either standing on her dignity or affecting nonchalance, two expedients Bice was equally incapable of, she was obviously not at her ease.

When she had explained how very sorry her mother was to be too tired to receive visitors, and how much she hoped to be more fortunate the next time Mr. and Miss Delorme were kind enough to call, she blushed and paused, and Mr. Delorme, naturally a quiet man, had to make the conversational running. He admired Bice's ornaments and curtains and pictures— everything but her books—in a perfectly sincere way, though he was making talk, and could not say enough of the garden, as he saw it from our windows.

"Such pictures as that are quite unique ; they please rather more than less after continental splendours," he said warmly, standing beside his daughter in the oriel-window.

"Would you care just to walk round?" asked Bice, half timidly, seeing his enthusiasm was real.

"So much," he answered, following her downstairs, without so much as a glance at Gyp and me; as though he had lived all his life—well, in heaven, instead of society—that realm of suspicion and caution and gossip and Mrs. Grundy. I wonder if he would have done it had he known how nearly my sketch was finished—as much of it, that is, as I liked to do at one sitting—and how soon I should be on a stool at Gyp's feet in the oriel, hoping that I had not tired her and kept her too long, and proposing that now we should talk over the *contadina?* I had got half-way through what, I will say for myself, was a very sober and sensible lecture on the art of water-colour drawing, when I observed that my pupil's attention was wandering. She leaned half out of the window to try and see as far as possible down the garden, and, that expedient failing, quietly rose to her feet, and looked out. I felt snubbed, and held my tongue. The silence roused her. "Pardon me," she said, recollecting herself. "What you tell me is good. At the next sitting you will go on, and I will listen well. For the moment I wished to ask of you something."

"Say on—unto the half of my kingdom," I muttered, rightly opining that I was securely obscure.

"I beg your pardon?"

"I mean only tell me, and I will do anything, or get anything, or go anywhere for you," I said breathlessly, though I tried to appear as off-hand as if I were saying no more than what was usual among ladies and gentlemen in English society.

But Gyp saw through me. Her rich colour

deepened, and a shade of something like embarrassment passed into her pure, still eyes. I hardly know why it emboldened me.

"Don't think me a ruffian for speaking out so plainly, Miss Delorme," I pleaded. "It's my way to come straight out with what I think, but it always *is* what I think. You may ask Bice. She will tell you I never paid any one a compliment in my whole life."

"Bice—that is your aunt," mused Gyp, rising once more to look out. This time she could see the two coming towards the house, engaged in animated conversation. Musingly, as though to herself, Gyp added, "My father says she is the sweetest person he ever saw."

"Ah, Gyp! Come down," called Mr. Delorme. "Miss Blake Johnstone has promised me a song."

"She sings well?" asked Gyp, almost anxiously, turning to me.

"Very well."

"What I wished to ask you was this," went on Gyp, hurriedly. "She does not believe. Nor does Mr. Edgar Blake Johnstone. I know of his writings, I heard him talk also. I see the books she likes. Already my father likes them too well, but for my sake he does not read them, and for my sake you—if you will indeed do something for my sake—you will help me to prevent that he ever shall. You will ask your uncle and your aunt not to speak to him of religion or of things that would make his faith to—tremble," pleaded Gyp, pressing her hands together, and trembling herself all over with unaccountable excitement.

"You may rely upon me," I cried, more careful to reassure than to correct her. She was so beautiful, I should not have cared if she had called me an infidel too, or requested me to become an immediate convert to Swedenborgianism.

Bice was half through her song before we reached the drawing-room. Mr. Delorme was—not pretending to listen—but listening.

When she had finished, he said a thing no other man could have said without making himself obnoxious. Without flattery, without patronage, without a suspicion of anything but child-like good faith, he said, "You have a very sweet voice."

"It is very kind of you to like it," responded Bice, quite as simply.

In the next song that he begged for, and that she chose to please him, there was a thrill in her voice that startled even me—used as I was to every inflection of it, to her sitting down to the piano whenever the fit took her and warbling bird-like ditties by the score in her musical soprano. It even took my attention off my Gyp for a moment, and as soon as the Delormes were gone, having appointed the day and hour for the next sitting amid many cordial speeches,. I said, all of a sudden, " Bice, it strikes me that our relation to each other is about to be transformed. You have already rightly surmised that Miss Delorme has done for me. Well, it wouldn't altogether astonish me to hear that you and I were shortly to become mother and son."

Blockhead that I was! I was excited, and full of hope and rapture. I didn't care what I said. I didn't see that I was doing what no woman would have been clumsy enough to do—what no man, even, with a grain of tact or delicate feeling, no man such as Delorme, for instance, would have done. *I* was happy. What did it matter to *me* that Bice was feeling now exactly as I had felt on that first day, when, if *she* had ventured to chaff *me*, I should have quarrelled with her? Of course I only know now how like a brute I had behaved. At the time, once the first tell-tale flush of startled sensitiveness over, Bice gave me no reason to suppose that I was paining her. She adopted my own bantering tone, and treated the whole matter as a joke, but I could tell by her behaviour from that moment that she was perfectly aware that if she had possessed herself of my secret, I had possessed myself of hers.

I suppose no one can tell what it was to Bice, after years of dull, monotonous, often galling and irksome home life, to see such a vista opening before her as she saw that afternoon—visions of protecting affection, and congenial companionship, and leisure and peace such as any woman must long for with a heart and intellect like hers—especially after considerable experience of the reverse. Of course Edgar and I had always been devoted to her, and I don't ask you to believe that such a woman could live to be Bice's age without inspiring more than one attachment of a tenderer character; but hitherto she had not seen any one good enough for her. Her opportunities had been few, owing to the secluded life she had led. I often pictured her in society, winning hearts by her graciousness, interesting gifted minds by her intelligence, pleasing all alike by the charm of manner which sprang from forgetfulness of self. But she was one of those "ornaments" not so very uncommon, I am told, that "society" has never had the chance of decking itself withal; whose names don't figure in the lists of presentations to her Majesty ; whose sweet fame has reached no "circles" beyond the small home-circle, which is consciously gladdened and unconsciously leavened by their presence.

It was not till the next day that I, with Gyp's curious, earnest parting charge tolerably near my heart, sidled up to Bice to tell her about it. Conscious of my blunder the day before, I was rather shy of approaching the subject of the Delormes, and I ask you whether it was an easy task to frame in polite language what in plain English amounted to this: "My lady-love having conceived an aversion for your (supposed) free-thinking tendencies, may I request you to confine your communications with your (possible) future husband to music and meteorology?" It is surely not very surprising that I made a thorough mess of it, and ended by frankly avowing that Gyp and I were a pair of young fools, but that I loved her to distraction, that I had promised her, and that Bice must do as she wished, or consign me to Hanwell.

"I wish my name was Golding," exclaimed

Bice, with her quaint look, as she turned from
me to replace an armful of books in the shelf.

"Oh yes, no doubt it's all a ridiculous, illogical
womanish whim!" I rejoined snappishly.

"Not altogether," Bice said, in her gentlest
though not quite her gayest tones, as she
studiously arranged her books. "Mr. Delorme
was telling me yesterday how very strongly she
feels on those subjects. He says she is not in
the least *dévote* in the ordinary sense, but that
she has an almost abnormal amount of religious
awe—a feeling of reverence approaching to
terror—terror, at least, with respect to irreverence and what she deems profaneness in
others. He thinks it a kind of disease; yet he
says it is too beautiful a disease not to respect
and yield to in everything."

After a pause for meditation on my little
darling, beautiful, as her father knew, in her
very negligences and ignorances, "Then one
may infer that he himself is not severely
orthodox," I said.

"If he is other than 'Catholic' at heart,"
Bice answered, "you may be certain of one thing
—that 'Gyp' will never know it."

III.

WHETHER Delorme reciprocated the feeling he had obviously inspired in Bice or no, it was evident that he was a good deal attracted by Edgar. Almost the next day he came over to have a long chat with him in the den, and made him promise to go up to the Hall as soon as he could, to see certain antiquities he had brought home from Italy on which he wanted his opinion. There were books, too, in the Hall library he wished to read while he had the chance; Edgar was to ferret them out for him; also to disinter for his benefit sundry curiosities in the way of family records, which he, Edgar, was fond of displaying to people of antiquarian tastes. Delorme was curious, too, about an ingenious little mechanical contrivance of Edgar's for illustrating the refraction of light—*que sais je?* There were endless points of contact and sympathy between the two—the patient, shrewd, and, I will say for the dear old fellow, modest man of science, and the equally modest, receptive, inquiring disciple of culture. I never should have fancied Delorme was the kind of man to make a good sportsman, but it soon turned out that he added a thorough-going British love of sport

to the rest of his accomplishments, having
indeed taken Altham principally on account of
the excellent shooting. I can testify to his
skill the few times I ever went out with him,
but unluckily I had to be a good deal away just
then on business connected with the nomination
before spoken of. Painting, writing, shooting,
Gyp, everything I cared for most had to be
tossed on one side for the sake of dancing atten-
dance on the horrid old man whose favours,
dating from the ugly, embarrassing and use-
less baptismal spoon and folk, I would gladly
have forfeited long ago, but for annoying the
poor old grandmother, who, apart from interested
motives, cherished obsolete ideas of the veneration due to the head of the family. There was
also a nominal examination to go through—and
there was, oh horror! there was the necessity of
looking up some place in or near town wherein
to fix my abode. I should be due there towards
the end of the year, some weeks before the
Delormes were to leave Altham ; and how was
I to tear myself away ? Only under one condition could the thing be dreamed of, namely,
that I carried Gyp's promise with me.

It seems difficult to believe it, when you think
what an insignificant, impecunious individual I
was, and what an admired, petted, rich, glorious

darling she had been from her babyhood ; but
as time went on, and I saw more of her, I began
to feel that it was not the utter dreary impos-
sibility I had once imagined that I should some
day gain that promise. I used to get more and
more of those long grave attentive looks, when,
bridling with a violent effort, the torrent of
passionate words that was for ever on the verge
of overflowing, I constrained myself to talk to
her of pictures, and books, and politics, and the
other half-dozen topics in which, like her father,
she took the curious interest of a semi-foreigner,
but concerning which, if I had a little more
technical information than she, she had immeasurably more sound instinctive knowledge than
I. At times, moreover, I noticed a certain
timidity and sensitiveness which did not seem
at all consonant with what I knew of the proud,
impetuous character. What could it mean but
the touch of the wonderful alchemist, Love ?
What could it mean but that she was yielding
to the power of my passion for her, to the fate
which if it had not destined us for each other
had at any rate destined that no man should
love her with the same absorbing ardour and
complete devotion as I.

I was not the only man she saw at the time.
Her father, though he seemed to have but few

friends in England, constantly had two or three
men as nice as himself down to shoot, one of
them a good-looking young fellow, the heir to
a fine property, and an old Roman admirer
of Gyp's. The pangs I endured whenever that
fellow came to the Hall I refrain from attempt-
ing to describe. He was so nice, it was impossible to help liking him, and Gyp was not a
bit more civil to him than to the rest; but I
can only say, to see her playing lawn-tennis on
his side, giving him his five o'clock tea, sitting
next him at dinner, talking Italian with him
at such a pace that I could never catch more
than a syllable or two out of the conversation—
the whole thing was a refined species of torture
I am very far from anxious to undergo again.
I'm by way of detesting jealousy too.

But I really believe I owe it to Campbell that
Gyp and I had any *éclaircissement* before we
parted. One Saturday afternoon, in October,
that I rushed down to Altham for the Sunday,
I found him there, for about the fourth time
since the Delormes came, and it made me nearly
frantic. He wasn't out shooting. Of course
not. Who *would* have been out shooting that
had only entered the glory of Gyp's presence
the night before, and saw a distant probability
of being allowed to pull Miss Delorme's wheel-

chair round the farm in the morning and read
"Tasso" aloud while the ladies worked or
painted all the blessed afternoon. No. When
I came in, having driven straight from Queen's
Stepping to the Hall, without so much as stopping to deposit my traps at the Cottage, I found
the beggar in one of the two splendid armchairs
that stood by the fireplace in the boudoir, and
Gyp in the other, Miss Delorme having been
recently carried upstairs. She had her work in
her lap, and her eyes fixed on his face; he was
holding up his "Tasso," and reading with limpid
purity of accent—

> "Vivi e sappi ch' io t'amo, e non tel celo,
>   Quanto più creatura amar conviensi."

I dare say he took me for Victor with the
coals; or he may have been too proud of his
reading to stop in the middle of a stanza for
Mr. Delorme himself; anyhow, I heard the
whole of those two lines, and noted the tone in
which they were delivered and the look with
which they were accompanied into the bargain.
Of course I was an ass to get into such a passion about it. Gyp's face, when she saw who
it was, ought to have been enough for me, and I
might have known that was only his exquisite
Italian that was fascinating her, but if—

> " To be wise and eke to love,
>   Is granted scarce to gods above,"

it is possible that a youth, an artist and a mortal, may be pardoned a degree of commotion on hearing his mistress made love to in her *mother-tongue* by an elder son with the charms of an Adonis, a finished manner, and an adorable temper. I don't know that I ever had to exercise so much self-command in order to speak to any one civilly. And of course he was as full of nice gentlemanly feeling and consideration for others as usual, taking upon himself to speak first, only because nobody else did.

"I do hope you've brought a better account," he said; "we have been so sorry for poor Miss Blake Johnstone."

"A better account of whom? What has happened? What do you mean?" I cried, looking from one to the other in bewilderment and alarm.

Gyp's eyes flashed something almost like reproach at me.

"Have you not been home? Of your grand-mother. Yesterday she had a seizure. In the evening there was great fear for her. Nobody could be sure—not the doctor even—she would not be obliged to die before night."

"And this morning?" I interrupted breath-lessly.

"She was better this morning. The doctor

hopes she may now recover, but she is weak—very, very, very," repeated Gyp, emphatically, as a kind of meagre English substitute for her native " *issima.*"

" I assure you all immediate anxiety is over ; I assure you you needn't distress yourself," said Campbell, earnestly, seeing me tremble all over, and *not* having seen me begin to tremble before he announced the bad news.

For sole response I glared at him wildly. He put it down, I could see, to the shock I had undergone.

Then I turned my back on him, and said pointedly to Gyp, " Will you walk with me as far as the lodge ? "

Gyp stared, and so did Campbell. I felt it. They both thought me beside myself.

" Yes, I will go with you ; I will get my hat," Gyp said in grave, slow cadence as she left the room. I saw her, with her fingers on the door-handle, exchange a significant glance with Campbell. Her eyes said, " He is unhinged, I must console him ; " her lips, " Mr. Campbell will be so kind to tell my father where I am gone."

Campbell scarcely answered her. He saw that he was not to accompany us, but could not see why, and he would have hazarded a

"Mayn't I come too?" if she had lingered a moment longer. To prevent his saying it to me, I flung out of the room, slamming the door behind me, with a gratuitous boorishness I blush to think of now. My rival, worth ten of me, was far too good a fellow to persist. He saw it was wiser and kinder not to follow, so he stopped where he was—a piece of good breeding and good temper for which I honoured him in the midst of my foolish paroxysm of jealousy and pain.

In a very few seconds Gyp was in the hall, and silently, with quicker steps than usual, we went out together into the park, where the bracken was yellowing, and the leaves were falling, with a chilly breeze whirling them about under a lowering sky.

I could not speak at first. I waited to be sure of my voice; to be sure, too, that there would be neither temper nor selfishness in what I was going to say; and while I was waiting, my companion timidly began her mission of consolation.

" Do not be so sad," she said imploringly. " Will you not believe that it is all well now? Last night, yes—but to-day—indeed, indeed there is no cause for distress." '

"Oh, my darling!" I cried, in my excite-

ment and agitation, thrown off my guard by
the new accents of tender, sorrowing compas-
sion. " I *do* believe that it is well since you
tell me so. It is not *that*. It's only that I shall
go mad if I hold my tongue any longer, and
don't tell you what my heart has been bursting
with ever since that day I saw you in the
garden—do you remember? when I begged for
the rose—see, here it is; you gave me others,
but I picked up this one that had been in your
hands, and it is mine, mine—— "

I stopped to press the withered thing again
and again to my lips. My breath somehow
forsook me. Even those incoherent sentences—
I could not go on with them. Only when I
glanced at her, and saw she had no words, and
that her face was one deep flush, I took courage.

" I will tell you why I speak so," I gasped,
with a bad attempt at calmness. " Because if
you *do* like him better, I mustn't see you again.
He is worthier of you in everything but just
one little thing—love—and if he—is chosen, I
—I shall not grudge him that beatitude. But
I can go to London earlier. I can go away to-
morrow, to-night. Oh, Gyp, don't think me a
selfish, brainless puppy! I shall never be able
to call much more than a few paltry hundreds a
year my own, and you are the heiress to—Heaven

knows how many thousands. I know how the
world reckons. But you and I, were we not
born for love, for art, for heaven, not for such
a shallow world, for such false delicacies and
hollow conventionalities? Away with them!
I am ashamed that I have let them weigh with
me for an instant. Will you have me, Gyp,
with my pride and my poverty and my faithful,
faithful love for you, or, must I go ?"

As I spoke I thrust my dead rose back into
its place, and seized her hand and kissed it
again and again.

Presently she raised her glorious eyes from
the ground and fixed them steadily on mine.

"I think," she said, speaking with great
deliberation, though her voice was not quite so
steady as her gaze, "I think that beneath two
different forms our faith is one. I think you
revere that which I revere, and believe nearly
what I believe. I have watched. I have
observed."

"And love, does love go for nothing?" I
interrupted, insane enough to be half impatient
with what seemed like calculation in her.

I shall never forget the lofty gesture of her
head as she answered, "Often in marriage *God*
goes for nothing. In *my* marriage that shall
not be so."

Still less shall I forget the lightning swift-
ness with which the loftiness and (almost) scorn
were swept away by a torrent of tenderness.

" Whether I love you ?—Whether I love you ?
Ah !——"

The rest was unspeakable, but the look she
gave me made my head swim, and I know that
she almost hurt me as she clung to me with all
the frankness of an English child, and all the
passion of a Southern woman.

Before, however, I had time to try and tell
her how happy she was making me, she had
sprung away from me, and was standing, holding
me at arm's length, looking over her shoulder
with dilated eyes and rigid features, and a fixed
hard expression that frightened me. The softer
mood had vanished as swiftly as it had come,
and though I was accustomed to these witching
variations of another clime and temperament,
though I loved her for her fire and impulsiveness
and sensibility, I could just then have spared
that abrupt transition to the Medea vein.

I soon saw what had happened. She had
seen her father coming through the trees from
the direction of the Cottage, and on his arm was
—Bice. They walked slowly, their eyes on the
ground, their lips moving in what looked like
intimate discourse ; at the moment I saw them

first they were stopping, and Delorme was bending over his companion, speaking with redoubled earnestness, and laying his left hand on hers—the one that rested on his arm.

I knew that in spite of all I could say, perhaps on account of all that in my selfish pre-occupation I did *not* say, Gyp had never been able to conquer her strange unreasoning antipathy to Bice, but I did not know till that moment to what an extent the feeling had been smouldering within her during the whole of our intercourse, gathering strength from suppression, increasing (apparently) instead of diminishing with time.

My eyes were opened then. There was absolute hatred in the expressive, wonderful face, as she turned it away from the two and set off at a quick pace back to the Hall.

"*You* will meet them," she said to me in a loud whisper as she passed me.

"Alas! what has she done?" I sighed, not expecting to be heard, not hoping to be answered.

But to my astonishment Gyp stopped short.

"*Done?* Have you not eyes? Do you not see that she tempts my father to—to—*love her?*" she almost hissed in my ear.

Before I could answer her she was gone. I stood perplexed and sorrow-struck. I foresaw complications more serious than any others that had threatened. If this blind, obstinate prejudice could not be uprooted, Bice's happiness would be sacrificed, that was clear. And could I marry the destroyer of it?

I raised my eyes and saw Bice colouring, and trying gently to withdraw her arm from Delorme's. Delorme, however, would not let it go. He faced me with an air of perfect unconsciousness; and with him the air meant the reality.

"Ah, Lance, you have heard all at the Hall," said Bice, clinging to my hand.

"See how pale and fagged she is!" Delorme said, looking down at her. "This is the person for whom we are anxious now. She has not rested for twenty-four hours."

"Oh, never mind me," said Bice, cheerfully. "The air has done me so much good, as I thought. Lance, Mr. Delorme so kindly looked in on his way home from shooting to see what he could do for us."

"And found the best thing he could do was to turn walking-stick. But we must not overdo it. She had been as far as her pet oak-tree, and now we must take her home. They won't expect me in just yet," added Delorme, after a momentary pause, during which he threw one backward glance at the house that sheltered his heart's delight and the mistress of all his actions.

"I wanted some one to back me," he went on, still looking down at Bice with a kind smile I should call paternal, if it were not unlike the man to assume even that degree of superiority over anybody. "I have been trying hard to persuade Miss Blake Johnstone to have a trained nurse down from an excellent institution I know of. It would spare her so much. She has no idea how much——"

"You underrate these Atlantean shoulders," interrupted Bice, laughing; "besides, she would so dislike a stranger."

"I agree with Mr. Delorme," said I curtly. "I know something about those shoulders, Bice, but you don't know what a strain this may be. You have always given in too much to her whims, poor old dear!"

"There, he takes my side, you see!" said Delorme, triumphantly. "Then you promise? You were *just going* to promise, you know. You will send for one when I get the address? My memory is so bad—but I know where to get it to-morrow morning at Queen's Stepping, and then you will write by the evening post. Is it a promise?"

I stole a glance at Bice's face as she answered, "I promise." The tone made me do it. It was so startlingly soft and sweet. As to the face, it glowed with a sort of ecstasy of gratitude for his sympathy and tender consideration. But he saw nothing unusual in her manner. Probably one must have been as used as I was to its *enjouement*, its constant brightness—I was going to say lightness—in order to do so.

"Have I given you all the messages with which my sister charged me?" went on Delorme, quite unconstrainedly. "How she will miss your visits, if you are to be detained much at home! You have been such a pleasure to her. It is such a pleasure to me when she gets any one she likes to be with her."

"Oh, I shall have time to come—often. I shall make time," smiled Bice. "I love to be with her. Did you know we had read nearly all 'Aurora Leigh' together? We are industrious when you are all out! We must certainly finish—— "

"When I am there," put in Delorme. "I want to know Mrs. Browning better."

By that time we had got to our own gate. Delorme let go Bice's arm, begging her to let the maid sit up, and get a good night's rest. Then turning to me, "Lunch with us to-morrow, if all goes well," he said kindly. I seized his hand and wrung it. I knew what he meant—for all his simplicity—by the invitation. I was overjoyed, of course, but I could not get over the scene I had just witnessed, and I continued the whole evening silent, moody, and irritable. I was mad enough to feel a kind of spite against Bice for having provoked the displeasure of my idol, and I answered her very shortly indeed when she asked me what was the matter. But she was not offended with me. On her way to bed (it was very late, but she did go to bed that night) she tapped at my door.

"Put out that light, you bad boy! I can't allow any midnight oil to-night."

"Why not, pray?"

"Because you'll be good for nothing to-morrow. And I shall want you to take a turn at the nursing to-morrow, perhaps."

"Stuff! You'll have Delorme's nurse down. By the way, come in, Bice; did he—was that what he was saying to you this afternoon in the park?"

"Why those knit brows, this inquisitorial mien?" asked Bice, with mock dignity, as she dodged behind my chair to hide her face from me.

"Bice, for heaven's sake, don't humbug now! You don't know what's at stake."

"At stake?" cried Bice, amazed. I turned round in my chair, and saw her clasp her hands in front of her, while her face paled and her whole expression altered. The next moment her arms were round my neck.

"Oh, my poor darling boy, you don't mean that she has refused you?"

"Thank Heaven, no, not that," I said.

There was a pause of several seconds. I was on the verge of telling her the whole truth, but, demented as I was, I could not bring my mind to that. She looked too lovely, and she was too tender and too gentle to be told by even a madman that she was hated.

"Oh, Bice, I've got a splitting headache, and I am not quite sure what I mean myself," I cried wearily. "*She* is so strange, you know; I had a sort of panic, lest you'd broken your promise about keeping clear of theology with Delorme. *She* has such strange fancies. I was only wondering what you two were so thick about."

"Mr. Delorme and I have never been 'thick,'" put in Bice, quietly. "He was only urging me about the nurse, and taking care of me, as—as—perhaps my father would have done."

"Do you mean that, Bice?" I said sharply with masculine brutality.

She was still behind me, but I stole another

look at her then.   It was very plain that she did *not* mean it.

" I wish you would be a little more open with me," I muttered sulkily, half disarmed by her confusion.

I felt her fingers wandering with a quick nervous movement among my hair as she answered me.

" Old boy, don't you know it places us women in a false position to own to sentiments which may never be reciprocated?" she said, with something of the old gaiety, though there was a quaver in her voice.   " Don't be hard on me! Don't insist upon my confessing that I'm dying for somebody who merely feels benevolently towards me!   I don't mind telling you one thing, Lance," she went on after a little pause. " I never knew before there were men like that. I never saw one.   He's very manly; he thinks a great deal, too.   And yet he has a mind like a child or an angel, I don't know which. It's just a being from a different sphere.   He looks at everything, as if he had come fresh to it, and he utters every thought that is in his mind, because—so it seems to me, at least—he never yet had one that was not reverent and pure and beautiful."

She drew my head back, kissed me on the

forehead, and hurried away before I had un-
said my cruelties.

But I could not sleep till I had been to her,
and told her that she was a trump, and that
I had not yet set eyes upon the living man
who was worthy of her.

IV.

SUNDAY morning dawned peaceful, bright, and
even hot. It was one of those rare days that
one gets sometimes on the skirts of summer,
a solitary jewel in the midst of a six weeks'
setting of cold and wet. My spirits rose with
the growing beauty of the morning. I was
friends with Bice, I was to lunch at the Hall,
our invalid had passed a comfortable night;
there was nothing to check the exuberance of
sanguine cheerfulness to which I was at all
times sufficiently prone. I went and wandered
about before breakfast among the flower-beds,
which were still a blaze of brilliant old-
fashioned scarlet geraniums, a feast to the eyes
amid the surrounding dismal hues of autumn.
How one does love a splendid colour when
one's heart is glowing with a hope as strong
and daring! I picked a lot of them and took

them up into the study. It was the first time
I had set foot in it. I glanced at the books
on the table. There was a volume of " Modern
Painters" magnificently bound. What did
Bice want with that again? I opened it.
On the fly-leaf was written, " Miss Delorme."
Next to it was a strange copy of George
Herbert, an author Bice knew by heart.
Again " Miss Delorme." On the sofa there
lay a pile of French novels, unbound, some
of them with torn covers. I had the curiosity
to search through *them* for a name. I found
—carelessly scribbled at the end of one of
them, in a foreign handwriting, " Giulia
Teodosia Delorme." Gyp's name was Giulia
—but not Teodosia; these were the books
her mother read and liked. I looked through
them. They were thorough trash, some of
them rather worse than trash. Presently the
door opened. I did not look up, thinking it
was the housemaid. But it was Bice. I knew
she was changing colour by the way she crept
behind me again.

" He lent me those without having read
them himself," she said apologetically. " He
said I wanted amusing, and he thought he
had something that would beguile a lazy hour or
two. He knew they had amused a lady once."

"That lady," I said, turning to the name and pointing to it.

"Ah, his wife!" exclaimed Bice. "That explains his look when he said it. It was that bitterly sad look he has sometimes."

"Has he never said a word to you about her?"

"Never. Has Gyp to you?"

"Never, though I have put out feelers more than once. I always thought the loss must be too recent, or they felt it too acutely to bear any allusion to it. But these books— *donnent à penser*, Bice. If she was the kind of woman to devour them—and they have been devoured——"

"Good morning, young people. Am I to pour out my own coffee?"

It was the bland voice of the anthropologist, who, hearing us talking, very sagaciously opened the door wide enough to insert his blond head and stop us. His coffee had often cooled before while we two were gossiping.

"I wonder if Campbell knows," I said to Bice, as we followed him downstairs. "He's known them for years. I'll ask him."

I made up my mind I would ask him on the way back from church. He and the other two men staying at the hall were not Catholics. They were sure to be at Altham Church, unless, indeed, Campbell preferred going to Queen's Stepping with Gyp and her father.

It was nothing unusual for me to be starting for church alone, as I did that morning. Bice had been a regular attendant there all her life until latterly, when the rector, a college boon-companion whom Jim had had the impiety to put into the living, made church-going pain and grief to her. We should none of us have quarrelled with the man's shooting and hunting if he liked it; but when it came to hearing our magnificent liturgy spouted Sunday after Sunday by an unprincipled mountebank in a theatrical tone that suggested nothing so much as a condescending patronage of the Almighty; when it came to listening patiently Sunday after Sunday to horrible medleys of effete superstitions, tremendous truths, and sickening commonplaces, delivered by a man who had never grasped—even intellectually— a single doctrine he propounded, or obeyed —even ostensibly—a single precept he inculcated, I say, I don't wonder that Bice turned restive. Her mother being Low Church, she had never been instructed in certain subtleties concerning the divisibility of the man and his office, and she now frequently took upon herself to stay at home rather than be tortured

beyond endurance by a discrepancy her very
senses were too fine not to be jarred by. I
dare say she read inspired authors there instead,
saying grace, doubtless, in her devoutedness,
before Milton or Spenser, as Charles Lamb
pertinently suggests. She had always gone
while my grandmother could go; but I suppose
there is a limit even to that marvellous feminine
power of self-effacement inconceivable by the
unassisted male intellect, and after a dozen
years of dreary, and another dozen of painful,
Sunday services submitted to for the sake of
her mother, Bice herself found it impossible
to submit to them any longer—for the sake
of Giles and Betty.

I was quite of one mind with Bice as far as
the spiritual edification of that kind of church-
going went; but I had a romantic affection for
the dear old beautiful building itself. I liked
the high pews, the ancient tablets, the very
fusty smell and tuneless grinding organ, for old
associations' sake, and as I had not so very many
Sundays at Altham, I generally went once.
Edgar sometimes went with me; but that
morning, possibly for an excuse, he had
volunteered to relieve guard in the sick-room.
He was by no means a bad nurse. His ideas
were shifty and to the point, his movements

noiseless and cat-like, and his mother clung to him a good deal. So Bice resigned in his favour for an hour or two, announcing at breakfast her intention of going up to the Hall to thank Miss Delorme for all her kind sympathy, and perhaps read to her a little.

"If you're there when they come in from Queen's Stepping, it will save Delorme sending word about the nurse," remarked Edgar, innocently.

I did not interfere. I knew Bice would do nothing of the sort. She was perfectly aware of Gyp's mania, and, for my sake, never encountered her when she could help it. Also she was apparently in the habit of paying her visits to Miss Delorme only when she knew she should not meet her brother. I dare say any woman could tell you why.

Well, I started for church alone. Campbell was not in the Hall pew, only the other two visitors—one of them, Delorme's solicitor, a grave, elderly young man, a connection of his, upon whom the sole conduct of a large business had accidentally devolved; the other a middle-aged diplomatist. I introduced myself and walked back with them to the Hall. They were talking of their host—or rather the diplomatist was. The other was listening.

" He should have bought an estate in England. What an ideal squire he would have made! A thousand pities he was driven to that roving, continental life. One thing, he made friends wherever he went, as many as Madame made enemies——"

There I broke in, " Did you know Mrs. Delorme ? "

" I had that honour."

" What was she like ? "

" A dream of beauty, but the devil of a temper, as you know."

" As I *don't* know. Then her loss couldn't have been the unmitigated grief to him one imagined ? "

The diplomatist started at me with the legitimate contempt of an intimate for a complete outsider.

" I never heard of it except as an unmitigated blessing," he said.

The lawyer smiled sardonically. But law and responsibility combined had made him prematurely taciturn. He said nothing.

Before I could extract anything more from either of them, the Hall carriage drove up.

" That's not the way from Queen's Stepping," remarked the lawyer.

" We've been driving round by the Cottage,"

called out Delorme, stopping the coachman.
" Saw no one but Bush. He said Miss Blake
Johnstone was out, so I left the address with
him. Get in, all of you. Plenty of room."

I got into the break with an anxious heart.
Gyp was opposite me, in crimson again, a
gorgeous combination of velvet and silk, that
would have annihilated an English girl of her
size, though it only made her look like an
empress. She was not at all constrained in
manner, as might have been expected after the
scene the night before; but there was no
knowing how she might behave to Bice after
that scene, and Bice, there could be little doubt,
had been detained at the Hall. I could not help
thinking of what I had just heard, as I looked
into the grand dark eyes opposite me. I loved
her madly. If she had inherited the temper of
a fiend, I knew I should love her all the same.
But that was impossible; I knew her too well
for that. There was a mystery—something
unexplained. She might be fiery, but she was
not cruel. She might be capricious, but she
was not mad. I made up my mind to a bold
measure; I resolved to make some pretext for
keeping her out of Bice's way when we got to
the house, and at the same time finding out, once
for all, the true cause of her exaggerated dislike

of her. Yesterday's behaviour meant more than dread of " unbelief " ; there was clearly some very strong personal feeling involved. But what could it be ? Why, if her father were really " tempted " to love Bice, should he not give way to the temptation ? Even Gyp, herself on the eve of marrying a Protestant, could not have seriously believed his salvation would be imperilled by a union with so sweet a heretic. I would question her frankly, defend poor Bice boldly, and set my foolish darling right.

Accordingly, when we pulled up at the door, I looked knowingly at the sky, and hoped it would hold up till the afternoon, as it was so long since I had seen the garden. My pretensions to weather wisdom were evidently not thought much of by the company, but for all that my hint was taken. Campbell suggested a turn now ; it wanted half an hour to lunch. "*You* will come ? " he added, looking at Gyp.

I pinned the diplomatist, who was following Delorme and the lawyer into the house, and as garden-walks do not admit of four abreast, and a very moderate amount of collusion serves to bring the right pairs together, he speedily found himself entertaining poor Campbell, some paces

in the rear of Gyp and me. He was a great
talker. The kitchen garden was lost upon him,
as he hardly knew a dahlia from an October
peach, and he would stop in front of its greatest
beauties, not to admire, but to tell a good story
with greater effect. I watched my opportunity,
and during one of these halts made a dive with
Gyp down the nearest nut-walk, and so out
of the garden into the shrubberies that skirted
the lawn. When we were alone together there,
she clasped her hands over my arm, as I had
seen her do with her father fifty times, and
looked up into my face with a mixture of
coyness and infantine delight.

"Bad man! You have run away from those
two. Is that courteous? But never mind.
You shall come with me. I know where there
is a rose; we will see if it can drive away those
serious looks. You sulk, because I left you
yesterday without ceremony; *non è vero?*"

How I came to be able to resist the fascination
of her smile at that moment I have not up to this
found out. Could it be that I had begun to feel
a little bit paternally towards her, as we do
when we detect grave faults in the women we
adore? (N.B.—We go on adoring them all the
same.) Anyhow, I continued to "sulk," as she
called it, contenting myself with kissing her

hands, and telling her demurely that that would
be too much presumption.

Then she changed her tone, becoming piqued
and puzzled. " I have offended you," she
said, disengaging her arm, and standing aloof
from me.

" Indeed—no," I said humbly but gravely.
" How could you, being all in all to me? But
you are right: I am sad. It makes me very sad
that you—do not love—one very dear to me."

" Your aunt?" interrupted Gyp, her eyes
flashing fire in an instant. " Ah! do not speak,
do not breathe to me of *her*. At first I could
endure it. I knew she was sister to *him*, the
man who talked blasphemies to me at Spa. I
knew she, too, like him, never went to a church—
see! she was not there this morning. That was
bad for my father, who is already too large in
tolerating people of no belief. But there is a
worse. While you have been away, I have
seen it, seen all myself."

" Seen *what*?" I asked in amazement, as she
paused for breath.

" Seen her try to make my father to care for
her," went on Gyp, breathing hard. Then
with a smile of ineffable scorn, " Oh, she is fine,
she is cunning; no one else may have seen it,
but I, who love him as my life, I have seen.

And she has succeeded. He is tender—oh, tender for her, as he never has been yet for any woman, even for me. I know him, he is good and honourable; he would not let her see his heart. But she has stolen—stolen it away from him, and it is wicked, wicked, wicked of her. She is false, hypocrite——"

She stopped short. Her passion was too strong for her, and she buried her face in her hands and sobbed.

I caught her in my arms.

"Don't, for God's sake don't, my darling, my darling!" I cried. I believe I had never seen a grown woman cry till then. "You are under some terrible—some absurd misconception. I can explain it all. I believe in Bice as I do in —you. Calm yourself—for my sake—and let us try to understand——"

But she tore herself away from me almost with violence. "I will never listen to excuses for her. I *know* it was her doing."

"And if it was?" I exclaimed desperately. "If she had the vulgarity, the unwomanliness— which I do not believe—to try and attract him, is it an unpardonable offence? Do not thousands of women commit it daily? Does it merit such hard names as you have bestowed on it?"

" What, you too ? " shrieked Gyp. Her tears were dry; she was all pride and fury. Then with forced calm and infinite disdain : " I thought the English were a moral people," she said superbly. " I thought here in England a good woman does not seek the love of a man bound to another."

" Your father is not bound to another; his wife is dead."

Gyp eyed me with a sovereign scorn. " You know that is a lie," she said.

It was my turn to be angry now. I should have retorted—yes, even to her, I should have retorted something she did not expect, only I remembered in time that she was but a child, a child, too, that had been nurtured among Latins, who teach the little children to lie in jest.

So, with an effort, I gulped down all my British indignation at the imputation, and only said to my poor angry child, " Hush ! I heard voices just now ; they will hear."

" Come this way," Gyp said, opening a door in the wall hard by. It led to the forcing-houses, of which there was an unusual number at Altham. " They will not follow us here," she added ; " I shall fasten the door. They shall not see my red eyes."

I followed her with rising hope. Though she was still in a kind of white heat of passion, I saw my way to deliverance.

She burst into the fernery, the nearest house to us, motioning to me to shut the door. I don't think she knew what she was doing. But the door was not closed behind us when we saw we were not alone. There, at the further end, half hidden by the glistening, feathery verdure, stood her father. He had just added a green spray or two to the bouquet of exquisite exotics in his hand, and he was giving it to— Bice. She was thanking him, with the sweet colour mantling her brow and cheeks, and the same ecstatic look that I had noticed yesterday, the look that spoke nothing personal so much as a profound delight in this fair creature of God. "Oh, thank you, she will be so very pleased," her voice was saying gently.

"Why, Gyp!" exclaimed Delorme, not confused, but seemingly a little vexed to see us. He had been annoyed by his daughter's conduct to Bice.

But it was not annoyance that was in store for him now. Gyp confronted them in silence, glaring at us all three in turn. Then with a wild cry she sprang forward, and clung about . her father's neck, gasping between her sobs—

" My father, my father, have pity! Let us go away from these people! Love me, love me —you must—for I will never see *him* again."

Her father tried to soothe her, at the same time glancing at me, anxiously, not reprovingly, for an explanation. I signalled that now was not the time to make it, and passing my arm through Bice's, led her quietly away. On our way home I told her as much of what had passed as I had breath for, but some instinct warned me to keep till the last what I knew must be a blow to her. It was only as we reached our own gate that I said sadly, " And, Bice, there is another cause, the principal one, for this jealous watchfulness of hers over her father. Her mother is alive."

Ten minutes later Bice came down to luncheon as usual. She was quite herself, and talked all the time to Edgar, to cover my despair.

I don't know how I got through the rest of the day. Towards nine o'clock, as I was lying full-length on the drawing-room sofa, wishing myself dead, I was startled by a ring at the door-bell. Two gentlemen were shown in. The room was dimly lighted, and it took me a moment to see that it was Delorme and Campbell. They had come, ostensibly, for the latest news of my grandmother; but I could see that

Delorme had something else on his mind. He moved about restlessly on his chair. At last he got up, and said, "Is your uncle in his study?"

I offered to send for Edgar, but he preferred going to him himself. Campbell and I were left *en tête-à-tête*. I wondered if he would speak first, and if so what he would say. He did not leave me long in doubt.

"Miss Delorme seems to have been very unwell all day," he observed, as naturally as possible, "but she's a little better to-night."

"Miss Delorme?"

"'Gyp.' You know she was ill before lunch? I've not seen her since."

"*Ill?*" I gasped.

He saw, even in the darkness, that I was alarmed.

"Oh, her father assures me it is nothing. I thought you would be glad to hear she is better."

"So I am; I didn't know it was—so bad as that," I muttered.

"Oh, it isn't *bad*," rejoined Campbell, cheerfully. "I fancy it's an attack of that mysterious ailment the French call *maladie de nerfs*. I never could quite make out what they mean by it. Her mother, you know, used to disappear

for days together, but, then, that was generally
an attack of something else."

" Temper ? "

" Well, yes, to put it mildly, temper."

" I had no idea she was such a termagant."

" But, of course, you knew that was the cause
of the separation ? ' Incompatibility of temper,'
only the expression is so mild for what he
endured, poor man, it sounds like satire."

" I thought she was dead."

" So does every one. No wonder they can't
bear any allusion to it. It's worse than a death,
isn't it ? "

At that moment Mr. Delorme and Edgar
came in. Edgar was not a good hand at social
manœuvring, and I saw in a twinkling that he
had been put up to what he was doing when he
lamely suggested to Campbell to come and have
a look at his den. The moment they were gone,
Delorme came up to me.

" I am so concerned for what happened this
morning," he said, in a grieved tone that was
quite new to him. " Very sorry for you, and
very, very sorry for the misunderstanding which
seems to be at the bottom of my poor child's
unfortunate resolve. But don't give up hope,"
he added kindly, laying his hand on my shoulder.
" She has a strong will, but she has a cling-

ing heart, too, and it is just possible that will conquer."

I felt a chill strike through me. I had been wretched, but I had not fully realized my position till I heard her father, who knew her best, talk of my salvation as a " possibility."

" As to the misunderstanding, I am puzzled," he went on. " I hadn't a conception you were not acquainted with my circumstances. I cannot now bring Gyp to believe you were not. Surely, surely you must have heard of them from Blake Johnstone ? The affair was, unfortunately, the talk of Spa. Indeed, I recollect asking him to mention it, to obviate any necessity for allusion to it. You see I shrink from that so. It has cost me—so much—suffering."

There his voice failed him.

" I recollect, we thought a letter of his got lost," I said.

He walked away from me, and arranged the books on the table. Then he moved to the door.

" *I'll* fetch Campbell; don't come with me," he said.

I obeyed. I could not have spoken very easily.

I noticed that he lingered at the door.

" Don't let Miss Blake Johnstone think hardly of my poor Gyp," he said—with an effort, I thought. " I value—I should have valued her friendship for her, more than I can say. You see she has had disadvantages that English girls have not—the quick Italian blood to begin with, and the wandering life, and worse than no mother. You'll say all that ? "

Before I could answer him, he was gone.

Oh, mother, mother-country! Land of freezing springs and dripping summers, of philistinism and Calvinism, of narrow brains and honest hearts, forgive my infidelities! You breed such men, and what you lack in colour, breadth, and life, you gain in loyalty, humility, and truth.

Late that night my grandmother had a sudden relapse, and the next day she died.

V.

WE had no longer any ties to Altham. I had to be in London; Edgar had no objection to living within easier reach of the British Museum and other sanctuaries of learning ; Bice, though attached to her early home, felt it home no longer now that its chief centre of occupation and interest was gone ; and the end of the year found us all three established in a little house in

South Kensington, where our joint incomes admitted of our living comfortably enough. I half forgot my troubles rigging out my new studio, a jolly little room at the top of the house, where I could let off steam in as many noisy, messy, irregular ways as I liked. I took up music at the time, (not content with scribbling and painting,) and spent a good many leisure hours learning the cornet. How was I to help it? Whenever I took pencil in hand I found myself drawing one face, and it made my soul sick, and time after time I tore the paper across the well-marked eyebrows or the firm lips, superbly curved, and vowed that I would never draw again.

We had not seen them before leaving Altham. Miss Delorme had written a kind note of sympathy and another of farewell to Bice, and Mr. Delorme had called once or twice when we were out. There seemed a tacit understanding that meetings were not desirable ; and as for Gyp, she took care that I should not even see her in the distance, though every instant I had to spare was spent prowling about the park or any place where she was likely to be, on the chance of winning, at least, a look that might give me comfort. They only had the Hall till Christmas. After that we should not have

known where they were if I had not met
Campbell accidentally in the street one day,
and asked him. He told me they had gone to
the south of France. Miss Delorme was not so
well, and had been forbidden to winter in
England. " I think I'm going there," Campbell
soothed me by announcing in conclusion.

I don't think I ever went such a pace in my
life as I did getting home after that, or had so
much to do to keep down the tumult of sore,
desperate feelings that struggled within me. I
rushed upstairs, three steps at a time, to my
cornet, and tried to exorcise my demons with a
kind of homœopathic charm, consisting of the
most fiendish combinations of sound ever conceived by the disordered human brain. I was
partially succeeding when Bice, with a horri-
fied expression of countenance, came in to
remonstrate.

" The neighbours will be bringing an action,
Lance. Do, for goodness' sake, stop short of
being a public nuisance, you most restless,
erratic, irrepressible boy. Come down and help
Bush and me to put up the brackets and things
in the drawing-room."

She stopped. She saw I was looking at her
with the peculiar expression people have when
they are thinking of *you*, not of what you are

saying. She put up her hand and pushed back her light brown, silky hair, laughing. "Is that right?" she said, slily.

But it was not her hair I was thinking of, though it never looked softer, or her dress, though its clinging black folds set off her slender form to unwonted perfection, or her womanly face, pink from the run upstairs, and full of youthful brightness, for all the trouble she had passed through. I was thinking of her bravery in bearing what was perhaps a greater trial than my own without resorting to any of my various expedients for getting rid of the load of misery. Or was I mistaken? Did she care so much after all? Should *I* have cared so much if I had been a woman? Had not Nature taken care that "woman's pleasure, woman's pain," should be less poignant than masculine emotions?

"Well, then, what *is* the matter with me?" asked Bice.

"I was only thinking if I should tell you something," said I.

She looked at me inquiringly for a minute, and read my meaning in my eyes.

"I'll decide for you. No, dear boy, you shall not," she said firmly.

"You don't wish to hear?"

She put her hand before my lips, laughing.

"Lance, you know you've often said I'm the only woman you know who never cared to find out secrets, and never told them when she heard them. Do you wish me to descend from my eminence? No!" There she looked up at me so comically, though wistfully, that I could scarcely help laughing, too. "Don't let's talk about any bothers now, that's a dear. Here's Bush come to know why I'm keeping him waiting."

"Please m'm, do you wish these here things done before I have to lay dinner?" panted old Bush at the door. He only intended a friendly reminder, not the shadow of a reproof.

"Oh yes; we're both coming, Bush. Mr. Lance is kindly going to help us out of our difficulties." And with that she dragged me downstairs, and insisted on my becoming violently interested in the hanging of two or three daubs of my own and the arrangement of a couple of shelves of *bric-à-brac*. What I was interested in was herself, her enigmatic behaviour, her quick graceful movements, her readiness of suggestion, and accurate eye (it was nothing but a *ruse* pretending to want me), her saucy smile (whenever she looked my way), the prattle she and old Bush kept up without inter-

mission. It was always good to watch those
two together. One of the most exquisite traits
in an exquisite character was Bice's manner with
servants and poor people and all inferiors. Not
only was it wholly devoid of even considerate
and benevolent patronage (and let no man think
that common ; it is, on the contrary, so rare as
to be scarcely ever met with), but it was absolutely humble, as it were apologetic for the
accident of birth, the hazard that sets blood
before worth, money before skill, and book-
learning before sense. You could trace the
vague influence of some such instinct in the
very tone in which she asked for what she
wanted in a shop, offered some delicacy to a sick
man, gave any trifling order to a servant.
With Bush, the dear old friend of our babyhood.
who had given us pennies to spend at the village
tuck-shop, and allowed us to make messes in
" his " pantry, her relations were, of course,
almost filial, and a good deal of mutual banter
would go on between the two on occasions like
the present; but neither from Bush nor from any
other subordinate did I ever hear uttered in Bice's
presence one word that was not consistent with
the reverence her very graciousness inspired.

To some such effect my musings ran, as I
lazily superintended her operations that winter

evening, stretched on a sofa, musing and gazing, while she hovered about, now springing on to a chair, now springing off it to consider the effect of her handiwork; now flitting across the room for a nail or an ornament; now dancing round it in triumph over what she had accomplished. It was to me one of those moments that come in great sorrow, when, for an instant, the atmosphere is lightened, and the clouds part, and you feel that love and hope are not dead in the world. When all was said, I had Bice. I had for my comrade, consoler, and confidante, a woman who was not only pleasant to look upon, and, as the Prayer-Book grandly puts it, beyond her fellows "adorned with innocency of life," but one of those buoyant natures that are gifted with all the sprightliness and elasticity which mortals in dejection know how to value; who, though they may not be unacquainted with grief, do not know what low spirits mean, being indeed, very probably, created chiefly with a view to the depression of sublimer souls. Then, and many a time afterwards, I realized my dependence on Bice, and I began to cling to her more and more. We were a good deal thrown on one another, as Edgar pursued an independent course of his own, and never went out if he could help it. All that winter we two went

about together, and now and then we had " good
times," and even hearty laughs over the way our
relation to each other mystified people. When
Miss Blake Johnstone and Mr. Golding were
decorously announced, and were presently heard
vituperating each other, or addressing each
other with the *sans gêne* of intimacy, people
would open their eyes in innocent amazement,
and for fun we used to carry on the joke, and
take care to say nothing that would betray we
were aunt and nephew.

At last spring came, and all the bustle of the
season, and London was transmogrified, and
exhibitions opened, and concerts began. I went
in for that kind of thing more than for balls and
crushes, to which Bice could not accompany me
on account of the mourning. I did everything
I could to kill time, and it was easier now than
in winter ; but I could not forget my dear little
Gyp. She was always in my thoughts and
dreams in her wonderful combination of passion
and gentleness, of maturity and innocence ; and
I never saw one woman among all the beauties
that flocked to London then who for one single
moment banished the recollection of her face. I
searched the *Morning Post* regularly for the
announcement of her engagement to Campbell,
and if I had one feeble shred of hope left at the

bottom of my heart, it was, I believe, owing to the continued futility of that search.

One morning in May—it was one of those notable days that are landmarks in one's life—when we chanced to be all at home together, Edgar electrified Bice and me by calling out suddenly, " By the way," in the middle of a poem I was reading aloud. Of course we knew the old boy hadn't been listening. He looked upon poetry as an ornamental appendage to existence with which he, personally, had but little concern, and seldom stooped to anything in the way of literature lighter than Darwin, Spencer, or Tylor. (How much that was heavier he went in for, I shall never know, thank goodness!) Still, it wasn't like him to interrupt anything we might be doing, and we both gaped at him in astonished anticipation of the startling piece of information he had forgotten.

Would you believe it? This is what he had forgotten—that " he had met Delorme in Piccadilly this morning." His estimate of the importance of the circumstance being so slight, and ours being so much greater than we either of us cared to show, it was some time before we could elicit more than the bare fact from him. He seemed to have ascertained nothing further than that Delorme's sister was much the same, and that his daughter was very well, and that they were living—by the way, he had not heard if they were all in town, but he was to dine with Delorme the next day at his club, and he would find out, if we cared to know.

If we cared!

About one o'clock the following night, I heard Edgar's slow tramp upstairs. The lights were out, and as I crept down to meet him I could see by the yellow rim round it that Bice's door was ajar. Then Edgar's candle effaced the rim. His room was next hers.

"Hullo, Edgar! What sort of a dinner did you get? What's been the topic? Evolution, or the telephone?"

"The topic," said Edgar with grim humour, "has been—well, I think I might say it's been Bice. The fellow seems more interested in her than anything else. But for that mythical wife you discovered, I should say he was in love with her. As to your young woman," went on Edgar, who fondly imagined that Gyp and I had had an unimportant flirtation, "you'd better go with us to the British Museum to-morrow, and hear all about her for yourself. I want to turn in now."

I reflected for a moment, then wished him good-night, and retired abruptly.

At breakfast I put out another feeler. No good. He had heard their address and forgotten it. He would take it down next time. Delorme had not asked for our address? He had not.

Nevertheless, he seemed anxious to meet Edgar. We were always hearing of fresh appointments, at the club, the museums, the Royal Institution. One day Edgar brought Bice a note from Miss Delorme. It was dated from a house in Queen's Gate. The writer was more of a prisoner than ever, she said. Would Bice do her "the *very great* kindness" of coming to see her at five o'clock on Tuesday afternoon? There followed a delicate intimation that the meeting would be *en tête-à-tête*.

" Poor thing, how she likes you, Bice! Of course you will go?" I said, handing back the letter to her, and swallowing the lump in my throat.

" Of course," said Bice.

When Tuesday came, I escorted her to the door. Victor opened it with a grin of recognition. He shut it upon me with another grin, as if it was a sort of joke shutting me out of that house. I walked up and down for the best part of two hours. At last Bice came out, and I joined her half a dozen doors off. I had not anticipated any difficulty in extorting information from *her*, and yet, though she talked as hard as she could all the way home, I found myself very little the wiser, at least as far as Gyp was concerned. She had not been very strong, and she was not engaged to be married—that was about all I got out of Bice. I informed her, sulkily, that, knowing my feelings, I thought she might have gleaned a little more information.

To see her eyes twinkling with fun did not improve my temper.

" If you don't behave yourself, I shall not mention her at all next time. I'm going again on Friday."

I was fain to be content.

On Friday I got away earlier than usual from the Office—I knew Bice's appointment was earlier. But, to my dismay, I heard sounds of visitors as I went upstairs. How long was she to be detained? I had the meanness to steal into the little back drawing-room, which was curtained off from the other, intending to ascertain to which category of boredom the callers belonged, the inert, the rattling, or the staying. I devoutly hoped it might not be the last.

The voice I heard was a very gentle one for a man's, a very well-known one, Mr. Delorme's.

Perhaps I shall be pardoned for having gone on eavesdropping.

"It is very good of you to say that," Delorme was saying. "The sight of me must be the reverse of pleasant to you, I fear, after last autumn. To think you have forgiven my silly, spoiled child! On your nephew's account——"

"Oh, it was only for Lance's sake one minded," put in Bice, brightly. "I know strong natures do form strong prejudices. Besides, I've more than once *suspected myself* of being a dangerous character! Come and see my ferns! They look well for London, don't they? They get plenty of nursing though."

I heard her dress rustling to the window. I knew their backs would be turned; so I put aside the curtain and looked at them. He had one of the tapering fern-fronds between his fingers. She was talking to him about it, carrying off what was certainly an embarrassing interview with consummate tact and self-control.

But Delorme was not thinking of ferns.

"I hope my sister will be well enough to see you by Sunday," he said, while they were still standing in the window. "When I found she could not to-day, I asked leave to bring the note on the chance of getting this opportunity of thanking you."

"Please, please don't talk about thanks," implored Bice, cutting him short again. "As if it could be anything but a pleasure and a privilege to do anything for—at dear Miss Delorme's request—to say nothing—— "

There she dropped her voice too low for me to hear the concluding words, and almost immediately after, Delorme rather hurriedly took his leave.

"Good-bye," he said. "You won't let me thank you. God bless you! Good-bye."

"Bice! What delicate negotiation are you conducting for Miss Delorme on the quiet?" I cried, bursting in upon her, before he was well out of the house.

For a second Bice winced—only for a second.

"If it's a delicate private affair of Miss Delorme's, do you think it's likely I shall tell *you?*" she said, drawing herself up with mock defiance.

I knew her too well to question her further. She had some good reason for her reserve. But my heart was nearly breaking, and I just went up to her as she stood by her ferns, playing with a particular frond, and hid my face in her neck as if I had been a schoolboy and she my mother.

"Oh, Bice, Bice, dear!" I said, "one is

only young once, and *you* understand. Don't
torture me by even pretending to take all this
lightly. Tell me seriously just this one thing,
only this—whether there's any hope of my ever
seeing her again ? "

" I'll tell you on Monday evening when you
come back from Altham," answered Bice, quite
seriously. (I had promised some neighbours
there to run down for Sunday.) "Perhaps I
shall know by then."

I thought, by Bice's face, that she did know
when she opened the door to me on Monday
evening. She had evidently been on the look-
out for me, and was brimming over with some
piece of more than usually joyful intelligence.

" Come in here," she said, pulling me into
the dining-room. "You are going to be the
happiest boy in the world."

" Oh, Bice! is it all right ? "

" More than all right. She has been dying
for you all this time, but her pride held out, till
her health gave way, and her father and aunt
took alarm. At last Miss Delorme decided on
writing to *me*. They paid me the compliment
of believing *I* could make all square. *I*,
the injured party!" repeated Bice, capering
with glee. "And I've done it. I made sly
advances the first day (you little thought I'd

seen her !) ; yesterday I fairly gained her over;
and to-day—well, I'll tell you all about to-day
by-and-by.   First, just run up into the drawing-
room and fetch me my——"

"Your *what ?*" I roared, stamping with impatience.

"Oh, very well, I'll go myself," said Bice,
meekly.   She had got to the foot of the stairs,
when I pushed her roughly aside and sprung
up half the flight.

"Your *what ?*"

"My last note from Gyp on the writing-
table."

I needed no more bidding then.   I darted
upstairs and into the drawing-room, and was in
the act of swooping down on a little mauve
pyramid there was on the blotter, when I heard
a faint exclamation behind me.   I turned and
faced a figure slowly rising from a low chair.
I felt my cheeks turn pale.   I know Gyp's were
death-like, and so much thinner than when I
saw them last that the eyes shone out preter-
naturally large, with an almost ghastly splen-
dour.

"Oh, I have frightened you!   Forgive me!"
I cried, trusting it *was* the fright.

"She said—you were—at Altham," faltered
Gyp, still with that fixed stare.

She had grown taller. Something had transformed her. It was the wraith of my rosy, rounded summer love.

" I *was* at Altham," I whispered, drawing a step or two nearer. " I went to the Hall to see your room and your summer-house and your rose-tree. I think it was the first happy moment I have had since last October."

" I have been unhappy, too," murmured Gyp, after a pause. " But this was the difference between you and me : I deserved to suffer. I injured one better—without measure better, than myself. I grieved her, and I grieved you. I behaved myself like a very little, very naughty child," gasped Gyp, her bosom heaving.

If I had known more about women, I should have known that stony look was the precursor of a storm of sobs.

And so it proved. The next moment she had sunk down again into her chair, weeping bitterly.

But such tears—what a solvent they are of all doubt, all constraint, all reserve ! I almost rejoiced in them as I bent over her, seeking to soothe her, imploring her to be as glad as Bice, and I, and all the happy world were now and would be for evermore. I noted how they brought the rich colour back to her cheek;

how they quickened her pulses; how they
melted her scared eyes into softness. I was so
happy, I could have cried myself.

But Gyp was not the girl to give way for
very long to what, in her eyes, was culpable
weakness. When she had relieved her heart a
little, she drew herself up in the old queenly
manner, put her handkerchief away, and smiled
at me as much as to say, "I defy you to make
me do it again."

She took me by both hands and made me sit
at her feet and listen to her.

"It is past now. I am quiet. Be good now,
and still, and hear what I have to say. You
still wish me to be your wife. Well! Will
you a wife who has these passions, these
tempers? For I have them still. I am of my
mother, of the South. If I see what makes me
angry—whether cruelty, whether sin, whether
want of faith—I must be angry. After, I find
myself wrong, as with your Bice. But at the
moment I must be angry all the same. Nobody
can cure me, not my adorable father, not the
darling *Zia*, not *you*. It is the blood. Now,
will you such a wife?"

She ended with a brilliant smile, as one who
was very sure of her answer.

"My father said, 'You will make a wild pair

of colts,' or something like that," she went on,
laughing.

"Did he? That's what Bice will say."

"Ah! Where is she?"

"Bice? Oh, never mind her. Come up into
my studio. I want to show you the most snug,
delicious studio in the world. Will you? I
have got some sketches and things to show
you. It is just perfect. It wants nothing but
the feeling that you have been there."

"Ah, yes! I shall love art again now. We
shall study together, paint together"—here she
clapped her hands for joy—" sing together, and
sometimes, shall we not *pray* together?" she
added shyly, as we were slowly, slowly moving
upstairs, and she was nestling very close to me.
" It might heal my impetuosity."

" I don't think I want it to be healed," I
mumured, much enamoured of her quaint speech,
more of her liquid eyes, most of her subdued
and childlike spirit.

We were both silent as we passed Bice's
room. The door was shut, but, as we lingered
on the landing, I could hear a sound proceeding
from it—a very unobtrusive, very unfamiliar
little sound.

It was Bice crying.

III.

A QUARTET OF QUEENS.

A QUARTET OF QUEENS.

I.

I DO not know that my feelings of trepidation at the idea of being presented to the Queens were in any degree modified by the reflection that they were my daughters. I am not even aware that I cherished the proper amount of paternal complacence in the fact that the four high-spirited, red-handed, gawky little girls I had left behind me in Ireland fifteen years ago had developed into four high-spirited, handsome, well-bred young women, who were prepared to welcome me as their father. The habit of living alone—and I had lived alone for ten years, since the most tremendous of all losses had so completely broken me down as to compel me to spend my short furlough on the hills instead of with my children at home— is well known to

operate rather singularly upon the social instincts; and I was no exception to the rule. I
may as well confess at once that solitude, and
possibly a little soreness of spirit, had imparted
something of a philosophical tinge to my reflec-
tions on the subject of my unknown offspring.
Especially during my last few years in India, I
had rather often caught myself wondering
whether, after all, the long talked-of reunion
would be productive of the intoxicating ecstasy
on both sides, which, in my softer moments, I
endeavoured to anticipate. What were the four
dashing young ladies of whom my sister wrote
me to make of a worn-out old Indian of sixty,
with a touch of liver, and another of irritability,
and an inordinate fancy for spending the best
part of the day in bookish quiet? The one
fact, that my excellent though original sister
Margaret invariably alluded to them by their
nicknames, and always talked about what the
Queen of Diamonds or the Queen of Clubs had
been doing, instead of relating the adventures
of Sabine or Harriet, filled me with appre-
hension. Commonplace girls seldom have
aliases—never invariable aliases. Mine, there
could be no doubt, were gifted with an inconvenient degree of individuality. Sabine, I felt
convinced, was ritualistic; Elspeth wrote novels;

Nina affected that cunning abomination, a frill of hair across her forehead; Harrie smoked cigarettes, and had only recently abandoned her practice of riding her aunt's ponies bare-backed. Nor would these and similar idiosyncrasies have received any wholesome check from Margaret. Margaret was a little bit " strong-minded" and a little bit blue, and had theories of her own on the subject of education; and I rather imagine that one of them was, that the best chance of developing a Madame de Staël or a Rosa Bonheur out of a British school-girl was to give her the run of an Irish estate, and let her ride ponies as Nature prompted, and crop her hair herself when it got in her way.

Then, what an example of insubordination she had probably set my daughters ! She had never chosen to be ruled by her husband, any more than by our parents or by me; and though there was some excuse for her independent view of the matrimonial relation in her having been betrayed into a *mariage de convenance* with a man in all respects her inferior, still it did not conduce to my comfort to reflect from how tender an age my young ladies must have been imbued with a similar view.   That they should acquire a salutary dread of any union in which respect, and consequently the only love worth having, could not be mutual, was quite in accordance with my opinions; but I did not relish their nurturing a too profound conviction of the superiority of their sex, and probably putting their principles into practice in the case of the first male relative over whom fate lent them undisputed sway.

But Margaret had settled that I was to live with them, and live with them alone. She had settled why—because I could "take them about." She had settled where—the neighbourhood of London—because they could be "taken about" in that region with greater ease. London itself, she knew, would not suit me. She was sorry she had never been able to do more than run them up to town now and then for part of a season, but even that she would not be able to do in future. The estate wanted a great deal of looking after, and she was getting old and creaky. She was not going to listen to any proposals for interring her brother and family alive in the wilds of Ireland. The girls had had enough of that. I was their natural protector, mentor, instructor, and chaperon. The Queen of Diamonds was six and twenty, old enough to keep house for her father. I might take them off her hands with her blessing.

Furthermore, Margaret decided that of all the suburbs the one best suited to our require-

ments was a place I chanced never to have
visited before I went out—Blackheath. It
was handy for London, she said ; and, besides its
being lively for the girls on account of its
vicinity to Woolwich and Greenwich, it was the
residence of a good many retired people I knew,
and should like to chum with.

Should I ? Thinking it over in the train, as
I was being whisked up to London, I came,
alas ! to the dismal conclusion that neither at
Blackheath nor anywhere else did I know of
any one that I should particularly care to " chum
with." I cannot describe with what forlornness,
having deposited my baggage at a hotel, I
sallied forth to the old club, whose threshold I
had not crossed for so many years, to order my
solitary dinner. It is true, I might have been
eating it at home, but something—weariness,
indisposition, perhaps that unaccountable mis-
anthropic shrinking from the novel phase of
existence before me which I have described—had
determined me to pass the first night—the last
night as my own master—in town.

It was a gusty March evening. A remorse-
less north-easter was levying its tribute of dust
even from the well-watered West-End streets,
and sweeping round the corners casting friendly
handfuls of it into my eyes as I walked, by way

of a welcome to my native land. I was not sorry to turn into the warm hospitable club dining-room. A less aggressive solitude reigned there, though it was still solitude. So, at least, I thought at first, as my eye wandered round the room and rested on nothing but strange figures and unfamiliar faces; when suddenly the tones of a voice from the far end of it reached me, and, without any figure of speech, transfixed me. True, the voice only called out for pepper, and that in a key denoting a rather prosaic amount of irascibility at being imperfectly provided with that condiment; but it was all one to me. I recognized the voice of the friend of my early manhood, Ralph Campion, and grizzled veteran, as I believe at this stage of my existence it is the proper thing to style myself, the sound of it made me feel very queer indeed.

I approached a few steps nearer to the man who wanted pepper. He had his back to me, and I was not surprised that I had not known him at first; he had grown so bald, and what was left of his black hair, now streaked with grey, was so thin and sparse and seemed so stubbornly disinclined to the pious task of help-ing to conceal the bare patch at the top. He was a good deal stouter, too. But when, by a judicious flank moment, I caught his profile, I

saw that it was the old Ralph. There was the
high massive forehead, the straight nose with
dilated nostril, the dark ample moustache and
smooth-shaven chin; there were the shaggy
brows contracting over the keenest eyes I ever
saw. I grew bolder now, and, advancing still
further, took a seat there happened to be opposite
him and looked him full in the face from time to
time, wondering if he would know me. It would
need his sharpness to do it. I knew that I had
altered greatly. I was bearded, white, and, I
believe, a little emaciated; and I suppose we had
not met for twenty years. And yet it would be
strangely unlike him if he did not. By-and-by
I noticed that he began to return my glances
with interest, and even laid down his knife and
fork to stroke his moustache—a gesture I knew
in him so well, so well. He did not twirl and
trim the points of it in season and out of season,
after the manner of the fidgety and the foppish;
but when he had anything on his mind, when
he was touched, when he was musing, when he
was glancing furtively at anybody who interested
him particularly—he would lay the palm of his
thin nervous hand upon it and bring it slowly
down over it two or three times in succession.
I was uncertain at first what sort of temper the
action might indicate now. It might mean that

he was beginning to recognize me. It might mean that he resented even so mild an approach to the critical "British stare." Ralph was always as sensitive as it is possible for any man to be without making himself ridiculous, and I have often seen the colour mount to his brow on occasions when no school-girl would have thought it necessary to blush. Possibly it did not altogether meet his views to dine under the not discourteous, but still pretty evident scrutiny, of an elderly loafer.

All of a sudden he rose, pushed back his chair, and came round the table towards me. His eyes were meeting mine steadily, but not a muscle of his countenance changed. I don't know that I can say as much for myself, as I noticed the limping walk that so vividly recalled the old campaigning days of long ago. He stood still in front of me.

"Fitzhugh, by Heaven!" he said.

I believe I said "Ralph," as I grasped his hand.

What we said to each other after that matters little. Enough that no two men ever met with more unaffected delight. We dined together, and sat up far into the night together, and when we parted there still seemed to be a world of things to say. Ralph was ten years my junior.

He came out to join the regiment in which I served some years as an ensign—a mere boy ; but even then I had never been conscious of any inequality between us. I had been, as indeed we all were in the regiment, fascinated from the first by an indescribable charm there always was about the man ; and after we had been through the Mutiny together, and I had nursed him through the wound that crippled him, and, as he was pleased to consider, saved his life, he was good enough to make me his chosen friend. Since then our lots had been cast in different places. At first we used to meet often and correspond regularly ; then we met often and corresponded irregularly. Finally, we neither met nor wrote. I did not know what had become of him, and I am not sure that he knew whether I was alive. But one thing I am sure of, and that is, that notwithstanding all those years of silence, notwithstanding the sluggishness of mind and slackness of pen, too often exhibited by modern Davids and Jonathans, not a day passed that I did not think of Ralph Campion and he of me. It did my heart good to feel that we were not to be separated now. He had been on the Staff some years, and, as the kind fates would have it, he had, so he told me, just got a fresh appointment at Woolwich, that is, close to

the home Margaret had chosen for me. We could
meet every day, if we chose. I should have no
occasion to hunt up Margaret's "retired people,"
who would infallibly bore me to extinction.

I went down to meet my fate next day with
a relieved and very much more cheerful mind.
Whatever happened, there would be something
to fall back upon. If I was ever in the girls'
way, or if the barometer marked squalls at any
time, as I had been told it occasionally did, even
in the case of grown up-young ladies, I could be
incontinently seized with a desire to go and smoke
a pipe with Ralph. That they would allow him
to come very often to smoke a pipe with *me*, I
dared not anticipate. Their heads would be too
full of their young sparks to admit of their
caring to do the civil to " old Colonel Campion,"
as a foreboding instinct warned me he would be
dubbed. But I felt that as long as I could flee
to *him*, my novel and perplexing lot would not
be without its mitigations.

Nobody met me at the station, as I had
abstained from telegraphing my arrival in
London. I had not been without visions of
the tableau Margaret, who I understood had
arranged to stay at Blackheath till I came,
would probably have got up on the railway
platform. I knew she piqued herself on her

immunity from the cringing dread of any public demonstration inherent in the average English mind, and could easily picture the *sang froid* with which she would have gone through the remarkable ceremony of introduction incumbent on her, in the presence of porters, guards, and passengers. I thought a good deal of myself for having stolen a march on her; and as I emerged from the station, looked about me for a vehicle wherein to deposit myself and my impedimenta in an airy manner, redolent of triumph.

There chanced not to be one on the stand at the moment; but before I had waited three minutes a cab came rattling up full speed, probably in the fond hope of catching the up-train, now puffing out of the station, and I made up my mind to take the place of the disappointed fare inside. The fare was a small creature, attired after my own heart in sober-coloured but perfectly well-fitting garments, light-haired, with no particular beauty to boast of, except a pair of cheeks as pink as almond-blossom, and the trim ankles, for which, in common with the majority of my sex, I have a special admiration. But she was young, and it was not at all in accordance with my notions of fitness that she should be allowed to scour the country in this way by herself. When I heard her say, " Oh, I've lost it," in a piteous tone to the driver, as she handed him his money, I am afraid I felt positively incensed against her parents or guardians for permitting such proceedings; nor were my pangs alleviated by the reflection that this was the style of thing I might expect in the case of the four Misses Fitzhugh. Society at home had made a stride or two of late years—that was clear.

I don't suppose I had the slightest business to address the young lady, but the little face had such a pained, perplexed look upon it, that on the strength of my white beard, I stepped forward, lifted my hat, and said, in the deprecating manner of a lion trying to do his roaring gently, "I see you have lost your train. Can I be of any service to you?"

In a twinkling the pink cheeks became crimson. My wrath mounted higher. A sensitive child like this to be allowed to travel about London alone! She gave me one glance, rather a searching glance, I fancied, before she answered, with grave politeness, "Thank you; I must wait for the next."

"Can I find out for you when it goes?"

Another glance, and this time she smiled as she answered, a little nervously, "Thank you. The truth is, a parcel was put into that train, and now there will be no one to claim it, I am afraid it will get lost."

"Let me come with you and talk to the station-master," I said. "Perhaps he could telegraph, and get it taken care of for you."

She accepted the offer, smiling her gratitude so sweetly that I actually found myself wishing that one, at least, of the Misses Fitzhugh might be something like her, in spite of the alarming modernness of her behaviour. We discovered that there were but ten minutes to wait for the next train; so having reassured her anxious mind about her parcel, I asked leave to wait and see her into it. I had my doubts as to the propriety of the step, but I could not somehow find it in my heart to leave her alone. She, however, seemed satisfied of my respectability, and, as we paced the platform to keep ourselves warm (March seemed more inhospitable at Blackheath than in London), began chatting with me quite frankly. I found myself becoming more and more fascinated; the little thing talked so playfully and yet so sensibly. She was not without the reticence a woman is bound to display towards an utter stranger, and at the same time she had none of the awkward air of constraint which I have sometimes regretted to observe in the most admirable of my country-women on less embarrassing occasions. She looked up into my face with the open bright confidingness which one scarcely believes in nowadays, it is so rare, even in children, and somehow it never occurred to me that she was probably an impostor. I confess that I was conscious of a slight shock when the charmer I had been longing to claim as a daughter incidentally alluded to the goal of her solitary journey. She told me she should often have to go up and down alone, as she had just got a reading-ticket for the British Museum, and being the only one of her family that had any taste for books, she did not imagine that she should often be indulged with a companion. Retaining my composure with an effort, I asked if I might venture to inquire what direction her studies would be likely to take that morning? She said that just now she was reading some of Milton's prose-works.

"And you like that sort of thing better than novels?" I rejoined, not without a sense of speaking like a more puerile greybeard than I was, and deserving the withering scorn I should probably incur.

But my bluestocking only broke into a merry laugh.

"Yes; as one likes dinner better than dessert," she said. "Good-bye, and thank you so much."

For the up-train came punctually in at that moment. I am sure the engine was more asthmatic and vulgarly noisy than usual; for I remember with what repugnance I was compelled to shout into her ear that I was very glad to have been of any use, and very sorry I could not escort her further. Once more she said, "Oh, I am used to it," as I handed her into the carriage; and I fancied—was it my fancy?—that her countenance fell for an instant; that a shadow of something like sadness was upon it; and that the shadow lingered long enough to tinge her parting smile.

I occupied myself as I drove to the address which had been given me as that of my own house in wondering what all those swift, subtle changes of colour and expression meant. Had the child a father, in India or otherwise? Had she an affianced husband? Had she a good mother? Or was she, as I rather chose to fancy, an orphan, a somewhat forlorn being with a heart-trouble hidden under that gaiety of mien and manner? I am aware, dear Mrs. Grundy, that I ought to have been thinking of no one but my own children at that juncture,

but I have already made a clean breast of the
reprehensible unconventionality of my sentiments on that subject, and throughout the rest
of this veracious history you must be pleased to
take me as I am.

The cab pulled up at the gate of a villa over-
looking the heath, having nothing remarkable
about it except its remarkable similarity to its
right and left neighbours. It was the sort of
house that always fills one with a lazy wonder
whether the occupants generally find their way
to it, or whether they, too, are not sometimes
ensnared by the marvellously ingenious uni-
formity of the whole terrace. I hid the cab
and luggage behind some . laurels, opened the
gate myself, ran up the steps—why had Margaret doomed me to a villa with steps?—and
rang the bell. The door was opened by a
model parlour-maid.

" Are the Miss Fitzhughs in ? "

" Yes, sir. Your name, please ? "

I had not intended to perpetrate a practical
joke, but when the woman flung the temptation
in my teeth——

" Colonel Smith."

" Colonel Smith ! " announced the maid to
assembled company in the drawing-room.

" Why, my dear Jim—— " began a feminine

voice in tones of surprised remonstrance, before I had shown myself. Then it was all apologies, flutterings, blushes, confusion. The voice belonged to a comely, well-preserved woman in the forties, whom I might possibly have taken for Margaret, only that I knew Margaret would not wear such a jaunty hat, and look so generally " up to date."

"I beg your pardon, I thought it was my husband," she said, glancing interrogatively at the other two ladies in the room. The nearer of these was seated with her on a snug sofa by the fire, and had apparently been assisting her in entertaining a couple of young fellows, who were standing staring at me on the hearthrug. There was no mistaking who she was. She was a great deal too pretty not to have been photographed a score of times in picturesque attitudes, with her hair dressed and her hair down, with a [sort] of St. Monica expression and a pert comedy one, in her everyday gown, and in her fancy-ball frippery. I had too many of these works of art in my own possession not immediately to recognize Miss Nina, the Queen of Hearts; but it was clear that she did not recognize me. She gave me a distant little bow, accompanied with no pretty blush, and looked as helplessly as her com-

panion towards the window on the chance of
the tall girl standing there talking to a tall
officer being able to throw any light on the
singular apparition of Colonel Smith.

The tall girl had turned round, and was
looking about her with a defiant expression be-
tokening some displeasure at the interruption.
She was handsome, rather than pretty, with
round brown eyes, a high colour, and a masculine vocal organ, as I found out when she
fixed her eyes upon me, and said abruptly, in a
kind of musical bass—

" You are my father."

" You are my Queen of Clubs."

I drew nearer to her as I spoke, took her rough
curly head in my hands, and kissed her forehead.
She submitted with a tolerably good grace, but
she did not blush either.

Then the Queen of Hearts got up and came
forward demurely to be saluted in her turn, and
make a little conversation. She had no idea I
should arrive so soon. Aunt Margaret had said
this *evening*. They never dreamed of such a
thing, or they should have met me. It was
most unfortunate. Sabine and Elspeth were
both out, and would be so sorry. She must
introduce Mrs. Lennox Smith.

Mrs. Lennox Smith bowed.

"Mr. Lennox Smith," went on Nina, indicating the youth nearest her, who was twitching the moustache he one day hoped to have with an air that indicated a degree of embarrassment at being the involuntary spectator of a queer bit of domestic drama.

"And Mr. Colquhoun."

"Mr. Desmond," said the Queen of Clubs in her turn, presenting her officer, a bronzed square-shouldered gunner, as I opined, with an honest, if a little bit sheepish, countenance.

A pause.

"What made you try and pass yourself off as Mrs. Lennox Smith's husband?"

This from the Queen of Clubs with sonorous sternness.

I was not a little staggered by the impeachment, and cast a deprecating glance at the alarming young person who uttered it, as I replied—

"Heaven forbid that I should contemplate such profanity. I never had the pleasure of hearing his name." Then, with a nervous fear lest my unnatural child had entrapped me into a *bévue*, I changed the subject by asking for Aunt Margaret.

Oh, didn't I know Aunt Margaret had left a week ago? Hadn't she told me she wished them to receive me all alone? She had gone off to the Channel Islands on Thursday, probably for the whole summer, and they were to say, if I wanted to see her in any hurry, I must take them over to join her there. It would be a nice trip for us all.

"Very nice," I assented, with a cheerfulness not wholly untinged with irony.

The stroke was so characteristic of Margaret that I felt how credulous I had been even to expect that she would be at home *en règle* to welcome me; yet I was not the better pleased with this fresh bit of gratuitous eccentricity. Her motives were excellent, no doubt, but it would have been, on the whole, more gratifying to me if she had abstained from placing another nine hours' tossing between her exercised and way-worn brother and herself. While my thoughts were following my sister in this not altogether bene-dictory fashion, my daughters' visitors were getting up to go. I heard a good deal of whispering, arranging, and apologizing, and it suddenly flashed upon me that my unexpected advent had thrown the day's plans into confusion. When I heard young Lennox Smith insisting in plaintive undertones, that "if it wasn't to-day it must be this day week instead," I could abide my *rôle* of untimely marplot no longer.

" *It* must be to-day," I said, "whether *it* be walking party, riding party, tea party, or missionary meeting. I will keep house till Sabine and Elspeth come in."

Nina and Harrie looked at each other in amused perplexity. The young men thanked me, and pressed them, and wheedled the chaperon on to their side, and ended by carrying off the three ladies in triumph. It seemed they were all to lunch with Mrs. Lennox Smith, and afterwards adjourn to an afternoon dance at the Greenwich College, where her hopeful son was engaged in adding to his maritime experience science.

"Sabine will be in directly. She will be very glad to get off going," whispered the Queen of Hearts to me, lingering behind the others a moment to pay this small tribute to the proprieties.

The Queen of Clubs had marched by in the reverse of an apologetic manner, as though feeling the importance of establishing no precedent in any way favouring undue paternal interference. I watched her, stalking on far ahead of the others with her swain. I saw, too, from my post in the window, how a sort of scramble for the right and left sides of the beauty took place between the other two gentle-

men, and how one of them, Mr. Colquhoun, I
suppose, recollected himself, and slipped back to
Mrs. Lennox Smith. All which when I beheld,
my spirit became as lead within me.

I had hardly unloaded and dismissed my cab
when the door-bell rang, and I encountered a
second tall young lady in the hall. But height
with Sabine was something different from what
it was with Harrie. In Harrie it meant robust-
ness, muscularity, the capacity (should the dis-
position exist) to knock you over. Sabine's
stature impressed you with nothing unfeminine
or athletic. It only gave her dignity, a certain
regal magnificence of mien which more than
justified her *sobriquet* of Queen of Diamonds.
She was beautiful, too, in her way, just as
Harrie was in hers, and I confess to a feeling
of considerable complacence as I beheld a third
handsome daughter in the stately creature who
came gracefully forward to receive my homage.
Perhaps, if I had had my choice, I should have
preferred a little less royalty and more spontaneity
about her greeting, a restlessness about her
chiselled lips, a tremble in her even, mellowed
voice—some token that I was more to her than
if indeed I had been Colonel Smith, with an
accidental right to chilly kisses. But when all
was said, she had received me graciously, which

was more than I, in my capacity of sexagenarian parent from India, had felt myself at all entitled to expect.

I discovered after a little talk with my first-born that she, too, had been intending to join the luncheon party and expedition to Green-wich, upon which I implored her, as she valued my peace of mind, to keep to her engagement and leave me to rest and look about me.

"Elspeth will be in soon, no doubt," I said; "and whether or no, you will greatly oblige me by going, my dear."

It seemed a great liberty, that "my dear;" I quaked as I uttered it, but I felt she might have thought me flippant if I had yielded to my inclination to substitute "your Majesty."

Well, if it must be so, she would show me my room and go.

I had somehow gathered, from what had passed, the false impression that Elspeth was likely to follow on her sister's heels, and would be home immediately, though she was not going out with the rest; and when an hour passed, then two, then three, and still no Elspeth, I was conscious of something very like disap-pointment. Perhaps I had professed more readiness to spend a solitary afternoon than I really felt (I have frequently noted a tendency

to make similar professions in persons of
advanced years, and have considered it a form
of pride); perhaps the sight of three of my
children had made me unexpectedly impatient
to behold the fourth. Anyhow, I was bored and
put out, and did anything but rest, as I prowled
about the drawing-room alone, taking up one
kickshaw after another—a photograph, a bit
of china, of glass, of mysterious work—to while
away the time.

What a drawing-room it was! How different
from the drawing-rooms of my youth! The
simple physiology of my childhood had taught
that we human beings needed light and cheerfulness as much as the potatoes that struggle
across cellar-floors to climb up to the window
opposite and get a glimpse of sunshine ; but
since then some high authority had clearly con-
troverted that naïve theory, and the main
aspiration of modern upholstery appeared to be
to shut the sunshine out as far as possible. To
say nothing of the quantity of curtains and
blinds that darkened the windows, an excessive
sobriety, not to say muddiness, of hue seemed
to me to prevail throughout the room, and I am
afraid I was Goth enough to contrast these
sombre tones and tints, many of them on the
verge of disagreement, with the cruder yellows,

blues, and crimsons of fifty years ago, in a manner not altogether complimentary to modern enlightenment. It annoyed me too, seeing a whole dinner-service of china inviting blows from my elbow, or the housemaid's broom in every corner of the room ; especially as pottery appeared to be at such a premium as to have beaten painting out of the field, and where there ought to have been pictures there were nothing but plates.

The twilight was beginning to fall over me and my griefs, and I had sunk into an arm-chair, and even, I believe, forgotten them for a few minutes, when the door opened softly, and there entered—Elspeth, the Queen of Spades ?— no; the little railway bluestocking I had been so romantic about in the morning, with the well-made gown and pretty feet, and cheeks like almond-blossom.

Could this be *my* little orphan ? Was *I* the caretaker she had seemed to need so much ? Might I call this treasure I had longed to father, without knowing whose it was, *my own ?* She hesitated a moment by the door, and this time she grew very white, as the smile she had had ready to greet me with trembled away into un-looked-for emotion. I seemed to read in her face that she, too, had been thinking during the day

of the morning's encounter, and I saw that the
recognition of her father in her friend of the
station was a shock.   Not a painful one, I
thought, but still a shock to an organization like
hers.   So I said nothing, but stood still where I
had risen, and held out my arms to her.   Still
she hesitated, long enough for the blood to come
back with a great rush to her face and go away
again ; still I waited, and presently she flew to
me and put her arms about my neck.

It was long before I had such another embrace from the timid maiden.   But, then, I
needed no fresh seal to the quaint friendship
which had literally sprung up at first sight
between me and my Queen of Spades.

II.

THE next day my daughter Sabine came to
me with a very important face to request an
interview.   I had already been installed in a
convenient den at the back of the house, which
arrangement suited the girls very well, as it
kept me nicely out of their way.   It also
entirely satisfied me, as I had conceived a rather
strong antipathy to the new-fangled drawing-

room, and could here enjoy my pipe and my books without being haunted by sickly blues and greens and superfluous crockery.

" I'm so glad you find it comfortable," quoth Miss Fitzhugh, as she came in and stood in the midst of my litter; but she spoke absently, and I could see that I and my comfort were not what she had come to talk about.

I watched her as she stood there, looking splendidly handsome, and just the least little bit embarrassed. It suited her well, this unusual hesitation, and I liked the half-humorous smile that flitted across those firm, shapely lips of hers too well to help her out of her difficulty. At length I relaxed.

" Is it about that letter in your hand ? " I asked.

" Partly," she said, handing it to me to read. " Kyrle is really very troublesome. I thought I had given him his *quietus* long ago."

Now I knew, and it had helped to frighten me of Sabine before I saw her, that she had refused her cousin, my young nephew Kyrle Fitzhugh, in spite of the baronetcy and £5000 a year. In my cynical opinion, a girl capable of doing that must be either very quixotic or very ambitious, and as the latter explanation accorded best with what I had heard of the

Queen of Diamonds, I had made up my mind that I was expected to look up something better for her—a Tory peer, perhaps, of severely orthodox religious views. Kyrle's letter, therefore, contained nothing that was new to me; only I had thought with Sabine that he had had his *quietus*, and felt sorry for the poor lad, as I read how his mother was plaguing him to marry Lady This and Miss That, and how he did implore and entreat his cousin Sabine to change her mind and save him all this bother.

"That isn't all," said Sabine, still with that humorous smile. "Nina and Harrie both had proposals at Greenwich yesterday. Nina gets them once a week; but this affair of Harrie's is more serious, and I thought you ought to know about it."

"Quite right, my dear," I responded in approved paternal fashion, though I was conscious of a sudden and unspeakable heartsinking at being thus ruthlessly plunged, ere yet my portmanteaus were unpacked, into the dizzy vortex of my daughters' love-affairs. Was there no escape for me? Couldn't they have confided in Margaret, or Mrs. Lennox Smith? Must they needs resort to a used-up old hermit long unversed in such matters, long untormented by domestic complications of any kind?

" Quite right. Harrie's affair is more serious. That means——" I queried hesitatingly.

" It means that she likes Monty Desmond very well, and that she has given him a good deal of encouragement, and that as he is very well off, it ought—one ought—perhaps to —promote it ? "

Sabine chose her words very deliberately, I thought. Was it that she felt the argument might possibly be turned round upon herself *à propos* of poor Kyrle ?

" Monty ? Monty ? Is that a son of Montague Desmond's of the —th ? Yes ? I know him well. A son of his ought to be worthy of a daughter of mine. Fancy old Monty having a boy that size ! "

" There's the ' *boy* ' now coming in," said Sabine. " He was to get his answer this morning. May I send Harrie to you, while I talk to him ? "

" By all means," I said. Thus cheerfully have I said, " by all means " to my dentist when he has suggested the extraction of a molar. "Only" —a pause—" what—am I to say to her ? "

My daughter " eyed me over " more in pity than contempt.

" What you think best," she said. " What you advise and think right."

" And *you* think he should be encouraged to have him ? "

" I think she is a wild girl, and would be far better married; but I believe she has decided against it—because——"

" Because ? "

" Well, because we three are for it," said Sabine, with a fresh touch of the humour which redeemed her composure from the frostiness it rather narrowly escaped.

" *My* best plan, therefore, will be to dissuade her ? "

" As you think best," smiled the Queen of Diamonds, retiring with as much haste as her dignity permitted.

My next visitor appeared in walking attire. Her short gown displayed a pair of what I can only call exaggerated " clod-hoppers." Her hat was perched coquettishly on one corner of a very untidy head, and her tie, as I believe she would call the thing round her neck, appeared to have been accidentally fastened underneath her left ear. She darted a defiant look at me as she came in, closed the door, and planted herself in front of me to be lectured. The bright, brown eyes said, " Do your worst " as plainly as eyes can; and I saw it was all the full, rosy lips could do to suppress an outburst of sarcastic laughter. The next moment, probably, she would be squaring her fists at me.

I put on an air of the utmost gravity; I frowned awfully, and after solemnly clearing my throat a few times, I thus began, " You're never thinking of marrying that young jacka-napes in the next room ? "

" Who's to stop me ? " fiercely retorted the Queen of Clubs, with an arch look that was irresistible.

" Certainly not your father, though he knows rather more about the family than you do," I rejoined with severe irony. " Certainly not your father. *I* presume to coerce *you*, my *daughter* and a *minor* ? No, my dear ; I know my manners better than that. The utmost liberty I shall take will be merely to inform you of my personal feelings on the subject; you will then be free to act as you think proper. Personally, then, I am wholly opposed to this marriage. Montague Desmond is a scatterbrains. His father was one before him. So was his grandfather. So more or less have been all his Hibernian progenitors. The rascal may have money enough to marry upon, but he won't have enough to live upon, as he understands it, if he is the man I take him for. And I wish you may not find that out to your

cost as soon as you are tired of his innocent
face and that wheedling insinuating brogue
of his. Now, off with you, and give him his
answer."

The brown eyes had opened wider during
the commencement of this address, and had
presently assumed an inquiring look, as though
it were not the easiest thing in the world to
make the speaker out. Was I in earnest?
Or was I making fun of her? By the end
of my speech this most bellicose young woman
had relapsed into defiance.

" And if I say ' yes ' after all ? "

" Don't be afraid of *me*," I said, deprecatingly, as I held the door open for her. " I
shall not visit it upon him. You will always
find me as civil, indeed, as amiably disposed
towards him as I am towards you at this
moment."

The Queen of Clubs strode past me in silence;
but she turned round when she had got into
the passage, and a pair of flushed cheeks glared
at me through the semi-darkness.

" Can't you be serious? "—in indignant bass
recitative.

There was something in the appeal that
touched me. After all, perhaps I was not
doing my duty by the child.

I was silent for a moment; then I said, in quite a changed tone, " Yes, darling, I believe I can be serious. Come back to me."

My daughter advanced a step or two and stared, this time in genuine amazement. Evidently she had not been accustomed to be spoken to so, nor, I am afraid, was it altogether an agreeable novelty to her; for she eyed me as suspiciously as a skittish animal coming to be fed, and sidled off into the furthest corner of the room for fear I was going to be more affectionate than she liked.

At that moment she heard herself called, and I have not the shadow of a doubt that she was very glad of it, and that, so far from experiencing any compunction as she marched into the drawing-room, she made up her mind then and there in favour of Monty. Three sisters to spite was good, but a satirical, mystifying old father to thwart was better; or, if she did not think so, I am mistaken in my notion of emancipated young ladyhood in general, and of my daughter Harriet in particular.

Somehow I found it rather difficult to resume my occupation of settling myself and my effects into my den after she was gone. A sense of what might be going forward in the next room was upon me. I suppose I got sentimental thinking over the magnitude of the issues at stake in that half-hour's colloquy, and calling to mind all that, thirty years ago, such a half-hour's colloquy had imported for me. We took such things very seriously when I was young. I paced up and down the limited space between my walls and my boxes till I was tired; and then, forsooth, I must issue forth and prowl about the passages, working off my restlessness as best I could. Somebody was playing a sonata in a sitting-room overhead, which drowned the other noises of the house, and it was not unnatural that, coming to the dining-room in the course of my peregrinations, and hearing no voices proceeding from it, I should conclude it was empty, and placidly walk in. What were my feelings to behold my third daughter Nina, looking dazzlingly pretty and mischievous in a big armchair, with young Colquhoun—not precisely kneeling at her feet, but quite evidently in the act of extorting his answer to a proposition which I had been given to understand was not of a character to require any definite reply! In my dismay I was about to beat a hasty retreat, when the young people themselves relieved me from all embarrassment by rising and welcoming me cordially.

" I'm so glad you're come," said the Queen of Hearts, with the most unconcerned air in the world. " Mr. Colquhoun was getting so tiresome! You know, he looks in here every day on his way to London, only he generally brings Mrs. Lennox Smith to chaperon him. He's her cousin, you know. He's trying hard to get into a business in London—ain't you? And meantime he's living with the Lennox Smiths. It bores him rather waiting so long, so by way of amusement he comes here and bores us."

Here Nina subsided into her armchair with a fascinating pout. Mr. Colquhoun, in no wise abashed, then proceeded to ask me how I liked Blackheath and the English climate.

Better than I liked him, I could have told him. His appearance was not unpleasing, and he had a very sufficient air of good breeding ; but there was a shade too little deference about him for my taste, rather too marked a tendency to overstep the line which separates self-possession from self-assertion. The section of young England to which he belonged is one to which I have always cherished a special repugnance, but I was consoled for his presence in my house by the reflection that he was pretty sure to become tired of frequenting it before long. The little flirt in the armchair would have none of him, I felt certain, nor did I regret the impending blow to his *amour propre*, knowing that the capacity of his kind for disinterested devotion is usually in inverse ratio to their opinion of themselves.

In my position, however, a moderate snub seemed indispensable, and I was considering how best to administer it, when the Queen of Hearts, abruptly—

"It's half-past four. Charlie ought to be here."

A fresh blow. But I was getting hardened.

"Who's Charlie?" I asked, without any visible emotion.

"Charlie Lennox Smith. He had a friend of ours coming down from town to-day, and he was to bring him at half-past four."

"Or was Davidson to bring Charlie?" put in Mr. Colquhoun significantly.

"As you like," said Nina, with an impatient toss of the head. "So that's why we've not been out yet. What unpunctual creatures men are! Suppose we three start without them?"

"I must be off," said young Colquhoun, whom the proposition did not seem to tempt.

"I'll look in to-morrow, with Colonel Fitzhugh's permission," he added airily, condescending to recollect that there was now a master of the house to be consulted.

"By all means, if you'll take your chance of finding us," I said, resolving to give Miss Nina a bit of my mind as to the propriety of our being "at home" on the occasion.

"Three in one afternoon—four, counting Desmond," I said musingly, when he was gone. "Is that your average per day, Nina?"

The creature burst into a witching laugh.

"About that, father. Say *four*—I think you might say four; for, after all, I've a right to count Monty. It's quite lately that he has taken to Harrie. He's a nice boy—our nearest neighbour in Ireland, you know. I hope Harrie 'll have him."

"And Aunt Margaret, is this the sort of thing your aunt—I mean, do young ladies of the present day—in short, is it quite as desirable as it is entertaining, Nina?" I blurted out, hopelessly incapable of the proper amount of severity towards the iniquitous piece of love-liness who looked as young and as engaging as when I had left her creating fictitious jealousies among her dolls.

I am afraid she saw I was melting. "Oh,

please don't," she said ruefully, rubbing her hand in a deprecating way through the row of little curls on her forehead. "It is so amusing! And there's nothing in it—really there's nothing in it, papa dear. I don't care *that* for any one of them."

"Unfortunately, that is precisely the ground of my complaint," I said, endeavouring to knit my brows into an expression of ferocity. I hope and believe that I should have proceeded with my lecture in a becoming manner had not the door-bell at that moment announced the arrival of Messrs. Davidson and Lennox Smith.

"I'll go and call Sabine," said Nina, springing out of her armchair. I fancy she hoped the move would dislodge me from my post of critical onlooker; and, in fact, it had the desired effect. Not caring to do the honours of my house by myself to more emptyheaded young loafers, I sulkily retreated in the direction of the den, leaving the dining-room to the undivided sway of the Queen of Hearts.

I had hardly closed my door when I became conscious that there was somebody else in the room—somebody who was three-parts buried in one of the roomy cupboards that formed the lower portion of my bookshelves, and contained, as my morning's investigations had revealed, all the odds and ends there was no room for anywhere else.

"Oh, I beg your pardon," cried Elspeth, withdrawing her blushing face from this convenient receptacle, "I thought you were out."

She stood before me, a delightful picture of housewifely busyness, in a great white apron with a bib to it, sleeves tucked up, and dusty fingers clutching the treasure just exhumed—a cookery book.

I suppose it was a whim of mine, but I thought her prettier at that moment than all the rest of them—than the splendid Sabine, the exquisite Nina, the brilliant Harrie. It must have been a whim, for in the matter of feature she narrowly escaped plainness, and if she passed muster with her sisters, and people did not stop to except her when they talked of "those handsome Fitzhugh girls," it could have been owing, not so much to her shape and her complexion, as to a sort of reflected glamour from the beauty of the others.

I made no direct reply to her apologies, but I took one dusty little hand in mine and startled her with the inapposite question—

"How old are you, my dear?"

"Twenty-four. Old enough to know how to make a pudding," she answered, with the

first return I had noticed of her gaiety at
the station, brandishing the cookery book in her
disengaged hand.

"And are these dusty fingers the same I
heard pounding away at a sonata just now?"

"The fingers?—yes. The dust is a more recent acquisition," laughed the Queen of Spades.
"I've been grubbing in the kitchen since."

"And when the pudding is made, you propose—— ?"

"Oh, then I shall get a good long spell of
reading, I hope, unless—anybody wants me."

"H'm. So you grub in the kitchen, do you,
as well as in the British Museum?"

"Well, the cook doesn't mind, and I like it.
I like to be doing something all day long.
'How doth the little idle wasp?'"

"Don't you ever go out?"

"Oh yes; I was out all the morning."

"And why was I not invited to go out with
you?"

The child looked a little confused. Then,
smiling upon me sweetly, "Everybody doesn't
care for stuffy cottages."

"Cottages! Well, and what next? How
many more occupations does the Queen of
Spades contrive to crowd into the twenty-four
hours?"

I spoke lightly enough—too lightly, perhaps
—for she seemed to think I was bantering her,
and the shadow I had noticed yesterday came
suddenly over her brow.

"You won't mind my being busy, will you?"
she said quite gravely, in a tone of plaintive
entreaty that went to my heart.

"Not if you will tell me why you are looking
so sad," I answered, as gravely as she, raising
the dear hand, dust and all, to my lips.

"Oh, not *now*—not *yet*," she cried, the colour
coming back again in its swift, impetuous way.
"I must——"

"Colonel Campion," interrupted the neat
parlour-maid, whose main *raison d'être* in my
house appeared to be to announce gentlemen.

One more welcome to my house it was not
likely that she ever would announce. Ralph
had indeed lost no time in fulfilling his promise
of looking me up, and I was so glad of it and
so boyishly surprised and excited that, long
after I had let his hand go, I stood gazing at
him for very pleasure, entirely forgetting the
amateur cook in the background.

I had indeed heard a sort of gasp that sounded
like "Oh, my cuffs!" when Jane put her head
in; but I should hardly have thought of Elspeth
again, if I had not been reminded by the direc-

tion of Ralph's eyes that I had omitted to
present him to her. Ralph could not say,
"Introduce me," but he looked it very hard
indeed, and I being so backward to my task,
up went his hand to his moustache—this time
in an interrogatory manner that had a degree
of rebuke in it, and instantly recalled me to my
senses.

"Elspeth, my dear, this is Colonel Campion,
a very old friend of mine. Ralph—the Queen
of Spades. You will pardon me the insignia of
royalty!"

"That pretty white apron?" said Ralph, in
his musical voice, with the graceful roll of the
r I always put down to his Gallic extraction.
That was all he said. He just looked at her
gently.

Anything more chivalrous in the higher
sense of the word than Ralph Campion's nature
I never met with. He was one of Elia's true
knights who reverence women as women, not
as beauties, or fortunes, or wits, or even be-
longings; and he looked at my little Spades in
her bib as gently as though for all the world
she had been the dazzling Queen of Hearts
herself. He took her all in in a moment,
from the crown of her insignificant head
to the sole of her pretty foot; and I could

see as plainly as if I had heard him mutter it that old Ralph was saying to himself, "I like that girl."

Many and many a girl had Ralph liked since I knew him first, and yet he had never married. Those who did not know him at all assigned selfish reasons for this; those who knew him a little were exceedingly puzzled by it. *I* had had no occasion either to blame or to wonder. I knew that hitherto he had never been able to bring himself to ask any woman to share what he considered the privations of a poor soldier's lot, and that now he was in rather easier circumstances, he fancied the time had gone by.

And doubtless with reason, I said to myself, as I saw Elspeth notice his limping walk and push a chair towards him with more than her usual alacrity. He seemed young enough to me—in mind, in spirits, even in face—his bulk and his baldness, notwithstanding; but to my children he was an old fogey; and the momentary castle in the air I built when I first saw him and a child of mine together collapsed before he had been in the room five minutes.

I divined that he would not relish having a chair pushed to him, and, in fact, he pretended not to see it, and went on admiring the apron.

He was exceedingly sensitive on the subject of his infirmity, as on most other points, and for the moment, I am certain, strongly objected to Elspeth.

" So this is your ' growlery?' " quoth he, looking about him over Elspeth's head, and deliberately seating himself on an unrecommended chair. " And a very snug growlery, too. I should like to share it sometimes when I'm off duty. When am I most likely to find you here ? "

" You'll find me here at half-past seven to-morrow, to begin with," I said, " when you will dine here, and be introduced to the other children. I fancy your sisters are not in the way just now, Elspeth ? "

" I'll go and see," said the Queen of Spades, with a quick movement that made me think I had startled her out of a rêverie. She did not, however, get to the door before Ralph had reached it, and opened it for her. I saw her glance at him in timid deprecation of the courtesy, and heard her say, " Thank you," as gratefully as if it had been her father stooping to be thus serviceable ; and again, I could detect, as Ralph hobbled back to his seat, that he was not altogether pleased. She was so long coming back that he said at last he could not wait any longer. He would come again next evening. I let him out reluctantly, and met Sabine on my way back to my room.

"I'm sorry I could not see Colonel Campion," she said; "but Nina thought it too late to go out, so I was with her and those men."

"What about Harrie and her visitor?" I asked.

"Monty has gone, and Harrie is on the heath with Sheila. She generally takes her out at this time. I haven't heard the result of the interview."

"And what have you said to poor Kyrle?"

"I have begged him to let the matter rest," said the Queen of Diamonds, her lithe tall figure growing an inch or two taller as she straightened herself against the wall of the staircase she had been in the act of descending. Then, with a touch of pique, "Do I understand that I am acting contrary to your wishes?"

"Not at all. 'She that wills not when she may' does not apply to the Queen of Diamonds. By the way, is it really true that that little girl Elspeth is twenty-four?"

"Quite true."

"And has *she*—ahem!—had no lovers?"

"Well, you see, she has been rather heavily handicapped, as it were," answered Sabine, shying a little at the slang expression she found herself reduced to. "She would have done very well indeed by herself, but with Nina and Harrie——"

"And Sabine——"

Sabine smiled the dignified ghost of a queenly smile.

"Besides," she continued, "Elspeth has never chosen to do herself justice. She's too learned for us. She's so reserved; and I fancy she's a little nervous, or something. At any rate, she doesn't appear to advantage before people."

"How can that be?" I said musingly, thinking of the winning little maid who had prattled away to me so unconstrainedly the day before. Was it that something in my patriarchal aspect had inspired unwonted confidence?

Enter, at the hall-door, with a bounce and a bang, the Queen of Clubs and her Scotch deerhound.

"Well, may we congratulate you?" inquired her sister, with the least suspicion of irony in her tone.

"Certainly, on a glorious walk," quoth she of Clubs, sonorously. "Here, Sheila! Sheila!"

Sheila manifesting a strong inclination kitchenwards, instead of following her mistress upstairs, Miss Harrie had to come down again and administer a pretty sharp manual and a very gruff lingual rebuke. I thought, as she passed me, that the flush on her cheek was too deep to have been occasioned merely by the March wind on the heath, and I also fancied that a degree of previous mental excitement was needed to explain the severity of poor Sheila's punishment ; but I knew better than to make any remarks, and for the next twenty-four hours we all remained in ignorance as to the terms upon which she had parted from Desmond. She would not explicitly deny that she had accepted him, and yet it was evident that she was prepared to box the ears of the first person who should suggest that she had so far compromised her maiden liberty as to engage herself to be married.

I told Sabine, before we parted, about the guest she was to entertain the following evening. I hoped she would have no objection. We could sit in my room, I added meekly, if he would be in the way.

The girls all seemed to think this not a bad suggestion, as I found out when the time came, and we were dressing for dinner preparatory to Ralph's arrival. I had begged for a small bedroom close to those occupied by my daughters, instead of the larger one destined me elsewhere, because—well, because the children had no mother, and I thought I should like it best so; and consequently I could hear most of what passed when they exchanged remarks in elevated keys through open doors.

"I hope that old Colonel Campion doesn't bore us to death to-night," I heard Harrie's masculine organ exclaim.

" Oh no. Sabine says papa's going to undertake him," answered Nina's pretty treble.

" Well done, the governor ! "—Bass subdued, but perfectly audible. "I hate prosy old men. I know I wish they'd both——"

Here I thought it only fair to give a tremendous cough. But it did not suppress the young ladies.

The next minute I heard—

" Mary ! "

" Yes, Miss."

" My old silk, please."

" Mary ! "

" Yes, Miss Nina."

" My muslin ; you know, that thing with the darn in it."

" Mary ! "

" Yes, Miss Harriet."

" My old yaller gown."

For Harrie, I grieve to state, did say *yaller*, and not *yellow*.

Dear me, what frights they will all be! thought I; but somehow, as they dropped one by one into the drawing-room, where Ralph and I were sitting, my inexperienced eyes wholly failed to detect any darns in the muslins or signs of decrepitude in the silks. They only looked ten times more resplendent and irresistible than by day; and I could see that the old fogey, in whose honour these despised though dazzling toilettes had been donned, was as unconscious of the compliment as I should have been in his place.

Even he, with all his long experience of life, seemed astonished at the grace and beauty of the girls, and scarcely concealed his admiration, as I presented him to one charmer after another. Elspeth herself, with her delicate colour and dainty white gown, looked as well as any of them, in my eyes, at any rate; and it was a proud moment for me when they grouped themselves over a strip of some sort of ecclesiastical tapestry in Sabine's hand, and my old comrade whispered to me what a lucky beggar he thought me.

That he should be thus " bowled over " was precisely what I had expected, but what I was not prepared for was the way in which the old fascination of thirty years since—to which I

personally had never ceased to be keenly
sensible—reasserted itself in my house that
night, ay, even before we had got into the
dining-room. It was an indefinite thing.
What Ralph said would not explain it, any more
than how he said it. He just sat there talking
and laughing with us; his fierce countenance
lighting up with kindness and content; his
enunciation slow and clear; his choice of
words happy and humorous—a hundred men
look and speak so without charming like Ralph
Campion.

But it was the old story. Before he had
talked five minutes, that gracefully poised head
of Sabine's, with a diamond in either ear, was
turned devoutly towards him; the tomboy's
brown round eyes were fixed on his, and her
fidgety limbs were still; the Queen of Hearts
forgot to look ornamental, and did look angelic;
and somebody who had chosen a chair in a
far-off corner drew it a few inches nearer to the
rest of us. There was no question of smoking
in the den after dinner. Harrie herself settled
that by saying imperiously as she quitted the
table, "Don't stay long, I want to hear the
end of that story;" and when, obeying her be-
hest, we followed her and her sisters ten minutes'
later, it was quite clear that we were expected.

Sabine and Nina were at work; Elspeth was playing a bit of dreamy music; Harrie was mounting guard over a low stool which she pushed close to Ralph's feet as soon as he was seated, commanding him, as only the Queen of Clubs or a child of five years' old could possibly have done, to " go on." The music stopped and the work was dropped, and once more we formed a circle round the " prosy old man," while he joked and chatted and held us all spellbound, just as I had seen him do scores of times in the old Indian days, when he was the pet of the station, and commissioners' and field officers' ladies fought for a place next the penniless lieutenant.

It recalled to me an expression of Goethe's I had met with in a recent stray excursion into German literature, *das Dämonische*—the dæmonic element, in the antique sense, there is still in certain people and things. How far Goethe was from intending any opprobrious suggestion in the term, such as it connotes to us moderns, is clear from his refusing it to his Mephistopheles. He meant by it, in the case of men, at least, that magnetic, mysterious ascendancy which science is incompetent to explain, that unaccountable spiritual royalty with which certain natures, otherwise undistinguished, are endowed; and

I am certain that if he had known Ralph Campion he would have applied it to him.

Suddenly, in the midst of a sally that so much diverted the unconventional Queen of Clubs as to cause her to throw her curly head back in fits of immoderate laughter, Ralph turned round.

"Might we hear some more of that pretty music?" he said slowly.

Elspeth smiled assent, and, seating herself at the piano, went on with the Andante our entrance had interrupted.

He went and stood by her, and would turn over all the leaves, though he must have seen that it was pain and grief to her; and when that piece was finished, asked for another and another, till Elspeth, blushing with pleasure, told him she really thought it was Nina's turn to sing.

"Miss Nina will sing by-and-by," said Ralph. He was a bit of a martinet, and he chose to have his own way, but he turned as he spoke to give "Miss Nina" such a smile, that I verily believe that young damsel would have willingly consented to be placed under his orders then and there for the rest of her life.

"Now, please, that *charming* air from '*Nabuco*' again," went on the old rascal, who had a *penchant* for operatic trash I never could abide. "That's charming, charming. I only know one woman who plays like Miss Elspeth. She lives in Guernsey"—Ralph called it Guairnsey, because he had to sound the *r*— "and I had some thoughts of going there in the summer to hear her. But now——"

"Now Elspeth will do instead," put in Harrie, promptly. "Oh, but I forgot! We're going there ourselves to see Aunt Margaret. You must come, too."

"Are we?" asked the Queen of Hearts, languidly, from out the depths of one of those capacious lounging-chairs in which she loved to frame her witching little form. "I thought they were such troublesome, savage places. I thought one had to land by rope ladders."

The Queen of Hearts was as ignorant as only a blue-eyed witch of one and twenty dares be. Nobody ever seemed to consider naïve remarks like the preceding other than enchanting, and it was evident that she expected Colonel Campion to be one of those gentlemen who thought her all the prettier for being vague as to the precise whereabouts of the Black Sea, and forgetting who reigned before Victoria. Nor was she greatly mistaken.

Ralph stroked his moustache with ineffable

content as he looked at her and told her what delightful places the Channel Islands were, and how much she would enjoy herself, once she had got over the difficulties of landing. Then he begged for a song, and listened to it attentively, though he did not conceal that it pleased him less than Elspeth's instrumental performance.

I have known Ralph frank almost to *brusquerie*, and another man behaving so would have wounded Nina's susceptibility. But when he said, "Wont you sing me something out of Miss Elspeth's ' *Nabuco*,' or, better still, that dear old ' *Voi che sapete*,' my favourite song ?" it was impossible to be affronted with him. The cajoling measured tones and graceful accent were irresistible, and the Queen of Hearts tossed aside the last new English ditty about the comparative merits of new and old loves to hunt up the "old fogey's" favourite song.

Later in the evening it seemed that he was most absorbed by Sabine, who had engaged him in an improving conversation, and seemed in a demure way to enjoy having her mind enlightened on the subject of the West Indies and tropical vegetation; and I couldn't help remarking to my old chum as he went away, that I hoped next time he came I should be allowed to entice him into the growlery, as in the drawing-room he was monopolized more than I approved.

" We shall see," Ralph said, nearly breaking his back as he stooped to pick up a ball of wool Sabine had let fall in rising—" We shall see what Miss Fitzhugh says. If she will have me, I'm not sure that I sha'n't stick to the drawing-room. There's only one thing that I like better than a yarn with you, and that is a gossip with the young ladies."

Ralph said this almost shyly, if I may say so of a man of the world. What I want to express is the utter absence of anything like common-place gallantry in the common-place compliment; the modesty of the man's mind, and the genuineness of his reverence for womanhood. He looked benignly round on them all as he wished them " Good-night "— a little more paternally perhaps than he would have done, if he had not just been flattering them, and they thought him what he was—the most captivating of mankind.

But I am glad they did not hear the irritable rogue on the doorstep a few minutes later, when he discovered that his " scoundrelly " flyman had failed him.

We were in the act of blessing the said flyman

together from the heights of the doorstep, and the March wind was whistling past us into the hall, when Ralph suddenly remembered that he had left his stick behind, and limped back into the house to fetch it. He could not lay his hand upon it immediately, for some one had correctly placed it in a distant stand, and I fear Elspeth must have heard a muttered malediction as she crossed his path on her way upstairs. Anyhow, she saw in a moment what he wanted, and, without pausing to reflect, she flew to the stand, pulled out the stick, and ran back with it to the six-foot hero of half a dozen battlefields.

I was watching them, and I saw Ralph crimson as he took it from her. She glanced up shyly for a smile, such as he had been distributing in the drawing-room; but all she got was an exceedingly stiff bow and a stiffer "Thank you." It pained me to see how her countenance fell; and when at last I had got Ralph off and was on my way to bed, I called "Elspeth!" in a low voice, at a venture, in case the child should be stirring. The next moment a slim figure in a blue wrapper stood in my room, looking very cold and shivering a good deal.

"Well, my little girl, forgive me for disturbing you," I said. "I don't know that I have anything special to say. I fancied we hadn't said good-night properly."

"Good-night," said Elspeth, as demurely as ever Sabine, presenting her lips to be kissed.

"Good-night, Queen of Spades, good-night. Stop a bit. What did you think of my old pal?"

"I thought he was much too easily offended," replied Elspeth, with decision. "I can't bear to see him doing things for himself, so I got him his stick, and he was very cross with me."

"He is huffy," I said. "You see, he has been a bit of an invalid ever since that unlucky wound. But he's a thoroughbred man, Elspeth, a trump, though you mayn't believe it."

The little blue ghost looked at me with a quaint, wistful expression, gave one more shiver, and vanished.

III.

WE saw a great deal of Ralph during the next few weeks. He came to our house most days; dropping in at odd hours, stopping often till abnormal ones; joining our expeditions to London and drives in the neighbourhood; sharing our daily interests; growing, in short, into the kind of inmate who, when he is thrown upon you, speedily qualifies you for a lunatic asylum ; and when he is welcome to you as the sunshine, becomes a part of your life.

The curious liking my daughters had taken to him the first time they saw him increased perceptibly every day. It would have been hard to say which of them admired him most, for they none of them said much about it, except Harrie, who, before a week was out, openly announced that she intended to marry him. Poor Monty was nowhere! Whatever his answer may have been on that famous afternoon, it must have been cancelled very soon afterwards ; for if ever meek, long-suffering lover endured a course of protracted, persistent, relentless snubbing, Harrie's lover was that man, once the Queen of Clubs had set her cap at Ralph Campion.

He used to come, poor boy, and have long talks with me in the den, opening out his honest, Irish heart to me till mine, dessicated and cynical organ though it be, bled for him, and I marvelled within myself at the strength of mind which could withstand—or the caprice which could feign indifference to such affection as that.

I fancy Sabine and Nina were just as far

gone as Harrie, their demureness notwithstanding ; for Sabine never happened to be out of the way when Ralph came in, and manifested a readiness to acquire solid information from him, surprising in one so habitually conscious of her own superiority ; and as for Nina, the giddy little goose rapidly became quite a reformed character. She found out that very young men, even when they adore one, send one superb valentines, and propose once a week, are, after all, more insipid than diverting, and though she had too much vanity left to give all her *soupirants* the cold shoulder, as Harrie did poor Monty, they somehow began to flock to the house less frequently, and in diminished numbers.

Elspeth's private sentiments on this subject, as on most others, remained more or less enigmatic. I could not believe that she was less attracted than the rest merely because she showed it less, and yet the child was so odd, I now and then asked myself whether her reserve really meant excess of sensibility, or whether it might not mean, as it is so often found to mean when it is unveiled, defective sensibility—the absence of any particular feeling about anything at all. Even when she was alone with me she seemed to grow more and more disinclined to open out to me. When we went up together to the British Museum—for she never went there by herself again—or to lectures or meetings in which she was interested, I used to try to get at her mind, but though she was often merry enough, she never would be confidential, and drew in her horns the instant I touched upon any topic more personal than the books we were exploring together, or the scientific experiments we had been witnessing.

It was in the least likely of all places—a ball-room—that I at length found out a little of what was passing beneath all that surface impassibility and preoccupation. Mrs. Lennox Smith, who, I should have mentioned, had been constituted the girls' chaperon by virtue of her cousinship with Margaret's husband, had vowed her dance would be a failure unless they all four came to it; so they all went, and I had the amusement of watching them the whole evening.

Elspeth was sitting near me soon after we arrived, and I was wondering whether the heightened colour on the mobile, intellectual face would not atone for its deficiencies of profile, and whether somebody would not come and engage her for the dance, which was of the deliberate, unexciting kind called " square," when I noticed the colour heighten still further. Somebody had just come in unexpectedly, and was standing by the door, sending a keen glance of inquiry through the room, and though Ralph's sharp eyes rested but for a moment on my child's sweet little head, I could tell that in that moment a world of tremulous feeling had been stirred within her; that she was astonished and over-joyed, and yet more than half frightened; I discovered, in a word, that she loved Ralph Campion with the ardent yet diffident love of a nature unspoilt by spurious excitement and the disastrous corrosion of fugitive attachments.

I said nothing. I wondered that Ralph, since he was not a dancer, did not make his way to us; but he remained stolidly at his post till the music struck up, and then, to my amazement, I saw him go and offer his arm to Sabine. He was not going to be shelved on account of his lameness. He could walk through a "square" with any man, and he chose to prove it that night, ay, and to dance with "the handsomest woman in the room," as he afterwards told me he considered Sabine. Sabine did look more than usually handsome. She had on some of her mother's diamonds, and she wore—what became her better than

diamonds and dignity — an expression of
singular animation, of radiant satisfaction,
as she glided through the dance with the
elderly, halting partner the chits of eighteen
were laughing at, and she would not have
exchanged for a Prince of the blood. Harrie
scowled at her with all the energy of which
she was capable, whisking past her as if she
would have very much liked to have accidentally
hurt her a little ; Nina, the sly puss, tried to
look prettier than ever, and sweetly unconscious.

It was the first time Ralph had provided
them with any sort of excuse for jealousy.
Hitherto he had been impartially partial to
them all, treating them as he treated no other
young ladies, but petting and spoiling all four
indiscriminately with that adroit combination
of paternal solicitude and chivalrous deference,
which I, from experience founded on Ralph's
history, have good reason to suppose to be the
shortest road to feminine favour. But that
his only dance that evening should be with
Sabine was quite enough to kindle all the
heart-burnings he had been so happy or so
wary as to escape before; and the fact was so
amusingly patent that, but for the graver
element represented by my earnest-hearted

Elspeth, I should have been inclined to call it the best comedy I ever saw.

A glance at Elspeth, however, as she sat watching the dancers beside me, very quickly diverted the mischievous current of my thoughts. She was playing with her fan very busily; her busy little foot was keeping time with the music; a sort of smile was about her mouth; there was something glistening on her eye-lashes. Involuntarily she turned her head when I turned mine. She saw I had seen the tears, and instantly her face and neck crimsoned.

"She and Ralph are a match for one another in sensitiveness," I said to myself; "only he is a tartar, and this is the gentlest of woman-kind."

But I was not going to let her off so easily. My opportunity had come at last.

"My little girl is not happy," I whispered; "will she never tell me why?"

I suppose that time I managed not to frighten her, for she looked at me very tenderly as she answered—

"I *am* happy. I have got *you*."

"But this——" I said, touching my eyelid. I did not care to let her see the joy I felt.

"Oh, I often cry," said the Queen of Spades, with a gentle laugh. "The others are so bright

and handsome, and clever—I mean clever in
society. I like them to be all that; but sometimes—I mean, till you came—I used to get so
very tired of—— "

" Of what, darling ? "

" *Of being the odd one*," she said, with a
pathetic smile. " Of course I might have been
more like the others; but I don't care for the
sort of people they do. Those idle men Nina
and Harrie like—I never cared for them much,
and Sabine's friends don't notice me. I had to
be very, very busy, because of being so lonely,
you see. But it's all right now."

" It's all wrong now," said our host, catching
up her last words as he approached us. He
was a thin, quiet man, a good deal older than
his wife, whose activity bored him a little.. He
had been a good soldier, and was now one of
Margaret's " retired people." " It's very wrong
indeed that you should be sitting down. I
must find a partner presently." Then to me,
" Your friend Campion is very active to-night.
Poor fellow ! What a fine fellow he is ! I often
feel tempted to regret his bravery. He wasn't
the fellow to be disabled. It's made him too
touchy. His mind's so young. I believe he
feels it at this moment as much as a school-girl
going to church with a patch over her eye."

" He should have married," quoth I sententiously, ignoring Elspeth. " He'd have been the better for the moral support of a good wife."

" No doubt his temper would have been all the better for it. He would have been taken care of, and not had to—swear all day at careless servants," Lennox Smith was going to say, only he did not think it quite polite to Elspeth. " By the way," he interrupted himself, " is it true that he resigned his patrimony in the quixotic way they say ? I've always wanted to know the rights of that story."

" Perfectly true," I said. " Like most men of the right mettle, he was a bit of a Radical when he was young, only his Radicalism took the not very usual form of practical, or, as you say, quixotic self-abnegation. As quite a little fellow, a child, he revolted against what he considered the injustice of primogeniture, the more so as he had a passionate attachment, he being the eldest son, to his next brother, a year younger than himself, and could not be brought to understand the grounds upon which one so immeasurably his superior—as he thought—was destined to a position in life so inferior to his own. The story goes that one day, when his mother was reading to him about Esau's sale of his birthright, and requiring him to take the orthodox

view of that transaction, the young freethinker
interposed with the energetic protest, 'But I
like him! I think he was a generous sort of
chap!'"

" *Was* his brother superior to him?"

The question came from Elspeth, though no
one would have said she had been listening.

"Not more able, but more intellectual. Ralph
himself was clever enough to appreciate his
brother's cleverness, which he did with all his
soul. I fancy he was about fourteen when he
made a formal request to his father to alter his
will in Hubert's favour, and finding him obdurate, ended by beseeching him with tears to
leave him the estate. (It was not entailed.) Of
course it was generally believed, and he was
told, that he would grow out of his folly; but
he was of the same mind in his twentieth year
that he had been in his fifteenth; and seeing
no other way of effecting his object, he ran away
and enlisted when he found his majority approaching. This step roused the paternal ire
to more than the desired extent; and though
the father afterwards bought him a commission,
and partially forgave him, he made Hubert his
heir."

"Quite right, too,". said Colonel Lennox
Smith. "The headstrong young rebel!"

" Hubert was a most cold-blooded, discreet, and admirable person," I went on placidly, as though every word we greybeards were tranquilly uttering were not going straight to my child's heart. " He was a good fellow, too ; and for a year or two he managed the estate as well as Ralph had foretold, principally to please him, only, unluckily, he died."

Elspeth gave a little start.

" Then who has it now ? " asked Lennox Smith.

" A son of Hubert's has just sent it to the dogs. Yes, it was a sad pity. The career of that young prodigal, his brother's hope and his, has been a thorn in poor Ralph's side ever since. It would have embittered a more long-suffering character to have a well-meant sacrifice turn out so, and I fancy it gave a fresh twist to that same *temper*."

" I'm going to get a partner," placidly remarked our hospitable host, upon whom the last half of my speech had obviously been lost.

" A degree of amiable absence of mind is excusable in hosts," I observed to Elspeth. It was my method of returning to the charge. " But I think that's an interesting story, don't you ? "

For a moment or two she could not answer

me. Then she glanced at my face with just
such an inquiring look as she had given me the
first day I saw her, when I accosted her as a
stranger. As she had satisfied herself of my
probity then, so, apparently, she satisfied herself of my sympathy now, for she met my eyes
steadily as she answered in a firm voice, though
her lips was trembling a little—

"I knew he was a noble man."

After that confession of her secret, Elspeth
and I said nothing more to each other on the
subject. Only, every now and then, when
Ralph was with us, she would sit closer to me
than usual, and oftener steal her hand into mine.

But I did not like the turn things were
taking. Especially I did not like Ralph's
marked admiration of Sabine on the night of
the ball and after it. He now began to pay
her so much attention as to drive the two
younger ones to strong measures; and one day
I discovered that the Queen of Clubs had
ordered Monty Desmond to come and console
her, and that the Queen of Hearts had given
notice that she intended to hold another *levée*
on such and such an afternoon. At this juncture I felt bound, for Monty's sake and my own,
ay, and for Elspeth's, to interfere. I wrote
to Guernsey, where my erratic sister was still

staying, to ask her to secure rooms for us in
the same hotel the following week; and one
morning at breakfast-time I announced, with
more authority than three months ago I should
in my wildest moments have dreamed myself
capable of, that on Thursday next we should
start for the Channel Islands.

The announcement was received with the
disfavour I had been prepared for. The Queen
of Diamonds thought June too early for a move;
the Queen of Hearts looked pathetic, and said
she did so love Blackheath; the Queen of Clubs
made a grimace, and vowed she would stay at
home. Nevertheless, Thursday afternoon saw
us all safely deposited in the Southampton express, exchanging spasmodic farewell speeches
with four gentlemen on the platform.—"Hope
you'll get down all right;" "Mind you let us
know you arrived safe;" "Don't forget your
promise;" "Give my love to Tommy," etc., etc.
The two nearest eagerest heads were those of
Charlie Lennox Smith, and young Davidson (it
is a curious fact that Nina's friends, like mis-
fortunes, never came singly); and peeping over
their shoulders was the bonnie Irish lad I was
so fond of, trying to catch his Harrie's eye.

"I won't see you when you come back; I'll
be away," he was saying in piteous accents

that would have melted anybody but the ada-
mantine Queen of Clubs, who merely drove her
hands into the pockets of the masculine gar-
ment she had on, and gruffly remarked what a
bore it was having to leave Sheila behind.

Behind him, again, stood old Ralph, stroking
his moustache. Apparently he came to see us
off for *my* sake, or for Sabine's, as he had
been talking more to her than to me, and had
insisted on piloting her through the crowd on
the platform, offering his arm in his irresistible
Grandisonian, old-world manner, and entertaining her, so she informed us afterwards, with a
humorous sketch of a night on board a steamer.

If she was sorry to part from her cavalier,
she did not show it, but soon after we were off,
pulled a letter out of her pocket and began
perusing it with a quiet smile. I could see, by
the tremendous hand—three words to a line—
that it was another petition from Kyrle, who,
poor beggar, had come down to see us a week
or two back without being allowed the chance
of making a verbal communication on the
subject nearest his heart.

Well, we were off! We had left them all
behind, the Queen of Diamonds' suitor, the
Queen of Hearts' courtiers, the Queen of Clubs'
devoted slave, the inexplicable, obdurate, repre-

hensible Ralph, and all the horrible complications
of the last three months. It was with a sense of
inexpressible relief that I paced half the night
through the deck of the steamer that was
bearing us away from so much disquietude,
mentally resolving that I would start fresh
when I got back again, assert my lawful
authority at home, keep all desultory male
visitors well in check, and even drop my
beloved old chum, if his fascinations threatened
to undermine my peace of mind.

In this resolution I was confirmed by the
sight of my dear Elspeth's sleeping face. The
active Queen of Spades· had managed our
journey for us, tackled Bradshaw, superintended
packing, provided refreshments and literature,
ordered about cabmen and porters, with an
appalling energy very nearly amounting to that
bane of the travelling paterfamilias, fussiness.
She had tired herself well, and was enjoying the
sleep of the just on the deck-sofa she and Harrie,
who disliked confined spaces, were sharing between them ; and as it was a mild, calm night,
even the inconvenient wakefulness of the restless Queen of Clubs was, for a while, suspended.

I had been laughing at the ludicrousness of
my own position, flying from the dozen or so of
men that were in love with my daughters, and

from the one man that they were all in love
with, but I did not laugh after I had squeezed
myself into the narrow space between my
children's berth and the next one, because my
Elspeth's expression in sleep had something in
it that touched me. I stooped to cover her better
with the rug that had half fallen off her, and in
stooping I thought that her face looked older
than it seemed by day. Her sweet skin and
mobility of feature made her look like eighteen
in the daytime; to-night she looked what she
was, in her twenty-fifth year, not less lovely,
to my thinking, at least, but very much graver
and more womanly; and as I called to mind
what she had told me of her life, and remembered all that I knew was in her gentle
heart, the thought that Ralph Campion or any
other man should, wittingly or unwittingly,
cause her trouble was more than I could bear.

The midday sun was pouring floods of golden
light on " the town " when we landed—not, to
the Queen of Hearts' astonishment—by a rope-
ladder. Margaret was waiting for us on the
quay, waving her handkerchief with all the
vigour of her character, looking indeed as if
she would have liked to tear off the large mushroom hat beneath which she had the strength of
mind to shelter herself, and wave that by one of

its broad black ribbons. No timorous, half-hearted matron she, who would glance around to note if other dames were wearing shady hats and waving ample handkerchiefs! She and her maid, too, were laden with sketching paraphernalia ; and she informed us, as soon as she could get near enough to kiss us all round, that she was not going up to the Hotel with us, as we should have enough to do eating, tubbing, and napping, but she had ordered a carriage to bring us in the cool of the evening to join her at Petit Bot Bay. We all made our salaam, so to speak, and watched her depart in a " chair," while we clambered into a larger and very dilapidated vehicle, which conveyed us slowly up the picturesque Avenue St. Julien to one of the best, most hospitable hotels I have ever seen. It had all the comforts of a private house, and was full of good company, and what with that, and the exquisite view from the garden, and the daily excursions to points of interest on the coast, and the splendid summer weather—to say nothing of the immunity from domestic care—I promised myself a very enjoyable holiday.

I am afraid the children would have thought differently, and would have got horribly moped, if they had not made, as usual, an instantaneous conquest of the whole Hotel—the whole island, I

may say—which, I confess, on account of its
ridiculous suddenness, diverted me nearly as
much as it did them. Mrs. Crossbie, Ralph's
musical friend, to whom he had given us an
introduction, and half a dozen natives Margaret
knew, had them to their garden parties and
picnics; and in a very few days Miss Nina had
turned the heads of half the officers quartered
in the island; and Sabine and Harrie had a
devoted admirer apiece, one of whom got mildly
snubbed, and the other vehemently encouraged.

"It's a *succès fou*," observed Margaret to me
one day, with her paint brush in her mouth, as
we sat together on some pointed rocks in one of
the prettiest bays in the place.   "Didn't I tell
you so? I always flattered myself I should
turn the creatures out pretty respectably! They
are not in the least really fast, only innocent
and unconventional—as I took good care they
should be—and too pretty by half. I couldn't
teach them to draw—that's all. But why, in the
name of wonder," she added, contemplating
with great complacency the sketch which was
worthy of her cleverness, "hav'n't you married
any of them yet?"

"For the simple reason," I rejoined meekly,
"that they seem more disposed to marry themselves."

"H'm. Well, maybe Mrs. Crossbie will save you the trouble. Isn't that she climbing up those rocks like an *ingénue* of seventeen showing off? Yes, indeed it is; and there go Hearts and Clubs after her with their retinue. Where are the other two?"

"I don't know," said I absently. My eyes were dreamily fixed on the calm transparent water. Margaret's were sharper; they were never fixed very long on anything.

"Why, that's Diamonds coming along this way!" she exclaimed presently. "Who's that lame man with her?"

Anything more unexpected and unaccountable than his sudden apparition in Guernsey, at our picnic, by the very side of his favourite, could not well be, but I did not need the keenest powers of vision in the world to tell that the lame man was Ralph. I jumped up to meet him.

"I see, Mrs. Crossbie kept my secret," he said slowly, as he wrung me by the hand, his face expanding with glee. "She asked me to come and see her, and I had the luck to get a few days' leave, but I told her not to tell you anything about it. Has Miss Elspeth heard her play yet?"

"I don't know. Where *is* Elspeth?" I asked,

for no other reason than because I was thinking it.

"Elspeth is very often discovered alone on
these occasions," said Sabine, smiling. "Shall
we go and find her? I think she disappeared
up that little path along the cliff."

"Don't *you* go, Diamonds," put in the despotic
Margaret, blundering egregiously for once in
her life. "I want you here. Let the gentlemen
go. Don't you see they want to talk?"

"Not at all——" began Ralph; but Margaret
was obstinate. Sabine had promised to try a
sketch with her that day, and she really couldn't
let her off again.

Charmed as I was to see my friend, I found
myself feeling a little bit cross with him as soon
as we were alone together, and I had had time
to reflect upon his whimsical, capricious, mysterious behaviour. After all, here was one of
the complications I had been so rejoiced to leave
behind me cropping up again, attacking me in
an unguarded moment, and betraying me into
pleasure where I should have felt nothing but
annoyance. When we had exchanged a few
nothings, "Don't let Margaret cheat you out
of your friend Sabine's company," I said, with
ill-concealed irritation. "Go and sit on the
rocks, while I hunt up Elspeth."

Ralph stood still and fixed a searching glance on my face. He said not a word, but his hand went up to his moustache in its most eloquent manner.

" Well ? " I said snappishly.

" I didn't come down here to see Miss Fitzhugh," Ralph said, in a steady, measured voice, still doing his best to look me out of countenance.

" You mean that you came down here to see *me*," I rejoined, relapsing under the old resistless spell into the most fatuous good nature. " Don't think me insensible of your affection, old fellow ; but look here, let me explain myself. My four girls unluckily share their father's infatuation. At this moment they're all four head over ears in love with you, and if you go on playing the mischief with their—I believe I ought to say affections, and don't immediately either declare yourself, or take yourself off, I'll be shot if I call you friend any longer."

Ralph stood still, listening to me with an amused smile. We had got half-way up the hillside, and from the place where we halted we could see Elspeth, sitting alone among the ferns, looking at the sea.

" *All four*," repeated Ralph, jocosely.

Wouldn't *all three* have been nearer the mark ? "

" *All four*," I persisted angrily. As I spoke, I saw a change come over Ralph's face.

It was only after a very long pause that he said, in a curious, unfamiliar voice, " What, Fitzhugh ! you wouldn't object to a shattered old scarecrow on crutches for a son-in-law ? Well, supposing I were to tell you I'd been proposing to that splendid girl, Sabine, to-day ? "

" I should answer that it was the proudest day of my life," I cried, with what I imagined at the moment to be genuine enthusiasm. I thought he was speaking the truth.

But the next moment my eye rested on Elspeth, and the momentary pleasure of the discovery that old Ralph loved one of my children became mixed with thoughts that caused me grievous pain. I suppose it was because my heart was full that I turned away from Ralph and became interested in the distant outline of Sark. I heard him mutter something about going to tell Miss Elspeth, and when I turned my head again, I saw that he was standing by her side. I was too sad at heart to join them. I sat down, to wait till they should join me.

I believe I waited there the best part of

an hour. What *can* they be talking about? And why doesn't he come back to Sabine? I kept saying to myself, and, after a time, I began to get impatient and uneasy and to feel that I hadn't got to the bottom of the mystery yet.

And then, all of a sudden, a light broke in upon me. I saw my *vieille moustache*, who loved wild flowers dearly, pull a bit of honeysuckle that grew close to where he stood, stick some of it into his own coat, then stoop and kiss the little hand in which he placed the rest. I had been too hasty. Ralph's choice must be here. My Elspeth was to be happy after all.

But I did not know for certain till night. We were all tired after the picnic, and I had gone upstairs early, but I had no mind for sleep. I suppose Elspeth, whose room was next mine, heard me pacing up and down, reflecting on the day's events, and anxiously speculating on the probable conduct of the three disappointed queens when the truth, if truth it were, should be made known to them. Would they drown themselves in the sea-bath next morning? Or would they, as I believed and trusted was more likely, philosophically console themselves with Kyrle Fitzhugh, Monty Desmond, and young Lennox Smith, respectively? I say Elspeth must have heard me prowling about the room, for she presently came in, in the blue wrapper, and said she wanted another " Good-night."

As I held out my arms to her, and she clung to me, pressing her flushed soft cheek against mine, and whispering to me over and over again that she loved me very very dearly, I did not need to see the spray of withered honeysuckle in her hand to know, beyond all doubt, that my heart's wish was granted, and that my dear old comrade had chosen the Queen of Spades.

IN MONOTONE:

A NOVELETTE WITHOUT A HERO.

IN MONOTONE:

A NOVELETTE WITHOUT A HERO.

———◆———

"Is there no stoning save with flint and rock?
  Yes, as the dead we weep for testify—
  No desolation but by sword and fire?"
                              Aylmer's Field.

I.

HER parents named her Stella, for she was born
to them in the heyday of love and youth, before
the star of their gladness set; and the horoscope
they cast for her was bright with all the hope-
fulness of inexperience and all the enthusiasm
of genius. Her father was a younger son, who,
had he lived, might have become a notable
painter, and so have vindicated his choice of
a profession which he was not encouraged to
adopt. Her mother was a singer—not his equal
in birth, but his peer in artistic feeling and

generous aspiration—partly German; a very
sweet, true woman. It seemed that, had she
lived, her soul might have supplied what her
voice lacked of brilliant qualities, so much true
histrionic instinct had she, so much of the
genuine sensibility which tells like magnetism
among even the dull and cold. But they both
died, he at two-and-twenty, of consumption; she
at nineteen, of a fever; and the baby, Stella,
was left. The circumstances of her parents'
marriage, as it were naturally threw the child
upon the care of her mother's family, and
accordingly she was brought up by two of the
singer's aunts, maiden daughters of a well-to-do
manufacturer.

The country town on whose borders these
ladies continued to live, even after the Factory
had passed into fresh hands, was, like most
country towns, quiet and clean, respectable and
gossiping. It was not without its charms, for
it stood on the slope of a peaceful and beautiful
valley, surrounded by well-wooded hills, and
watered by a clear little river—clear, that is,
until it got past the town and into the meadows,
where it was tainted with the factory dyes. This
river flowed through the Miss Warrens' garden—
before it reached the Factory, understood—and
in the summer-time roses and tall lilies mirrored

themselves in its pure depths, bending in unrestrained luxuriance from luscious velvet banks.

It was the summer time when Stella Marryot attained her mother's age—nineteen—and such a summer! In the early part of it abundance of wet—afterwards uninterrupted sunshine for weeks together—everything growing madly—you would have said it was not England. Stella would go out every day to savour this rare season. She would stand among the roses to breathe their sweetness—perhaps to worship them a little. In the end of June, when there were not only roses, but hay and strawberries in the air too, and a languid twitter of birds, and a rich haze, and a busy murmur of insects, this child who had been much alone, and very often sad, was almost happy.

She stood on the morning of her birthday beneath the great willow that overshadowed the stream where it passed into the garden, dreamily swaying one of the lithe branches to and fro. From this post she could see, without herself being much exposed to view, what went on on the road. She could see the laden hay-carts rumbling by, the farmers going past in their lighter vehicles, the tradesmen whisking along; at this time of day, the postman, stopping probably to exchange salutations with a friend.

Would he bring Stella a birthday-letter to-day?

Yes! No! Yes!

Her heart beat faster as she heard the click of the latch. The hand with which she took the letter from him was cold. The address was in a clerk's copperplate hand-writing—although one would have thought—well, no matter.

And the note ran :—

" MADAM,

"It would be quite impossible for us to let you have the guitar, second-hand, under the price named, £7 7s.

" We remain, madam,

" Yours obediently,

" DEICHMANN & Co."

Poor little madam! Impossible to remember her dignity and prevent the swift tears from rushing to her eyes; for in this guitar lay her last hope, and she had only been able to save five pounds out of her allowance. She must not play the piano much—hardly at all—because Aunt Catherine was old and a nervous invalid. True, there was the church organ once a week; but what is once a week? Imagine a smile once a week! Now, a guitar one could take into the garden, out of hearing of neuralgic patients, or into the woods out of reach of precise, patronizing rectors. A guitar would be one's companion, and confidante, and confessor.

"A guitar would have been very precious to me," sighed Stella, like the *gemüthlich* German damsel she was at heart, spite of English bringing up and a parentage three-fourths English; and then, to keep the tears back, she lifted up her voice and sang, to a melody of her own finding, with a shade more emphasis than usual—

"Nur wer die Sehnsucht kennt
Weiss was ich leide."

"Stella! Not quite so loud, Stella dear!" called a voice from the drawing-room window. And as Stella's too thrilling tones died away into silence, there emerged from it Aunt Sarah, the younger aunt, of sixty or so, with the iron-grey curls, and rosy, healthy-looking cheeks; with the short grey gown, frilled collar, and cameo brooch.

"Who is your letter from?" asked Aunt Sarah.

"Only about that guitar," said Stella, just a little wearily.

"And of course you can't get it for £5. It wouldn't be likely. Perhaps, next year——"

There Aunt Sarah paused and seemed to be trying, mentally, to reconcile her principles with her kindness of heart.

"We must hope Aunt Catherine will be better," she said, at last. "I should like you to keep up your practising. But a guitar—I don't see how you were to learn to use it, to begin with."

"I thought perhaps I could learn it by myself —with a book," ventured Stella, a strain of sadness in her voice, and a little pout—not a naughty one—about her mouth. "And you know Mrs. George Head used to play it a little when she was young."

"Mrs. George Head is entirely given up to the Zenanas," said Aunt Sarah, primly, without an idea of anything jarring in the remark.

"I wish—— " began Stella.

"Well, what do you wish?"

"Something stupid. I wish the house was bigger."

"Because of the piano not being heard? Well, but, dear Stella, as I've said so often, you make too much of it. I want you to remember that school-time is over now, and that it's time to be doing something for others. Why, what would your great-grandmother have said to a girl wanting to be playing and singing all day?

Why, at your age I was in the kitchen a good part of the morning, and waiting on my dear mother the rest of the day. Though she was not brought up a Friend, she had a good deal of sympathy with my dear father, and it shocked her to hear the piano in the day-time."

"Not in the evening?" interrupted Stella, quite seriously.

"Oh, she liked it in moderation and at proper times. I remember she was very fond of Corelli's jig. Dear soul! I have heard say she was one of the last people to give up her spinning-wheel. I can remember she liked to spin of an evening while we played or worked. But what are you going to do to-day?" asked Miss Sarah, abruptly. She was of too practical a turn to waste much time over reminiscence. "What is the birthday-treat to be? Shall we drive over to St. Julyans to see the Loan Collection, or shall we have the Marshalls in to tea and a row afterwards? I'll send a note now."

"I think," said Stella, flushing violently—"I think I should like my birthday treat to be—I mean, do you think if I went to Mr. Marshall and told him it was my birthday he would let me have the organ to-day as well as Friday?"

"You can but try," said Aunt Sarah. "But it's a foolish choice, I think."

And so it was with a burden of disapproval upon her that Stella set forth on her quest, a sense of depression, discouragement, and discontent with herself.   She was so fearful of giving umbrage that it had cost her a great effort making this last piece of folly known; only one thing would have been harder to her —to give up music for that day.   Her thoughts were all remorseful as she threaded the white, bright streets of the little town, at the other end of which the Rectory stood.   " Aunt Sarah would have liked that Loan Collection.   Oh, I am selfish !   I have made a selfish choice ! "

This was an artist's nature, and one of those that are young and tender always, not only in young and tender early life. Such have barely the self-assertion necessary to those who strive for the mastery in things beautiful. They need that to them much should be given, for they will die (not metaphorically) before they will take much.

There was one house in the main street of Astlett that Stella never passed without a sort of shudder. This was Savin's, the linen draper's, whose shop had more than a local reputation, and who had made a good thing of retailing the woollen fabrics manufactured by Head Brothers. That house sheltered her dearest foes, the Miss

Savins, two dressy, forward, rather clever girls, whose ill-governed impulses in the musical direction had been the cause of her practical exclusion from the organ. They tormented the Rector for the key of the organ, lost it when they had got it, bullied the pew-opener, left the organ open, one day damaged the bellows, till at last Mr. Marshall, who dared not take stronger measures because Savin was his churchwarden and stanch supporter, had to make that safe general rule about the Astlett ladies having access to the organ on one day only in the week. It could hurt nobody's feelings, and—well, who would have thought that it could help to break somebody's heart ?

Mr. Marshall was a kindly but precise person, one of those men who succeed in making themselves awful without being particularly strict and without ever losing their temper. He had a negative way of not welcoming suggestions, not embracing new ideas, not fostering spontaneity of action or feeling that chilled you. If you mentioned a new rose to him, he pursed up his mouth and looked grieved. You were not sure whether he was reflecting with regret that his own gardend not boast that rose, or whether he merely objected in a general manner to excessive enterprise in floriculture. If you asked permission to infringe routine in any way, you got no remonstrance, much less any reproof, but you got this dreadful expression of countenance which was worse than either, and proved a more useful weapon than he knew to this amiable, methodical, rather nervous man.

Stella's lively imagination pictured that look as she asked if Mr. Marshall was at home, and for a moment she felt almost relieved to hear that he was out for the day. But was the desired permission to be obtained in his absence ?

"I simply daren't," said Dolly Marshall, who had spied her in the doorway and heard what she had come for. Dolly was the eldest of the rector's motherless children, a useful, sensible girl. "The Savins would be sure to hear of it; and whether they did or not, I should get into trouble. I'm *so* sorry, Stella. If only our piano could be any use to you, I'd soon get it dusted; but it hasn't been tuned for about a year, and it would make you ill!" laughed Dolly, who did not come of a musical stock and could not hum "God save the Queen" in tune.

The very mention of the rectory piano sent a shiver of pain through Stella's nerves; but she tried to smile and said, "Oh, if I could not get the organ, Aunt Sarah said, would Kate and Agnes come and spend the day and have a row after tea—and Ernest too?" added Stella, glancing in the direction of a long-legged fellow in the uniform of the Merchant Service who was smoking in a hammock.

"I don't know that I can spare them all," said Dolly, good-humouredly fishing for an invitation. "Father won't be home till late; and Tottie has put off coming back till Tuesday."

"Oh, you must come, too! I beg your pardon. I know you generally don't—I—I was so sorry about the organ," faltered Stella.

"I'm dreadfully sorry too; but come, cheer up, you mustn't take it so much to heart as all that!" Dolly said, shaking back the crisp brown curls that covered her whole head and showing a row of gleaming teeth. "Why, the river to-night will be fifty times jollier than all the organs in England. I'll get Charlie Head and the Harrisons to meet us at the bridge, and we'll get up to Bun Island—see if we don't!"

"I was stupid to show Dolly what I felt," thought Stella, as she trudged homewards under the noonday sun. "She must think me very silly. *She doesn't know about the guitar.*"

II.

"How *could* your Aunt Sarah let you go on the river last night?" asked Aunt Catherine, in the middle of Stella's morning kiss.

Aunt Catherine thought all time wasted, even kissing time, that was not spent in repining, remonstrance, or reproof.

"I'm very sorry my cough disturbed you," said Stella, who had learnt from long experience the best method of parrying the complaint indirect.

"But the rain!" said Aunt Catherine. "The torrents of rain! Weren't there torrents of rain last night?"

"Not till after we got in."

"And Bowder's dog! I thought Bowder had *promised* to silence that dog! Stella, do you think it could have been the thunder that set Bowder's dog howling as he did the whole of last night?"

"I think it must have been; he's been quiet so long."

"Indeed, he hasn't been quiet. Nothing's quiet in this place. Stella, how *can* you say Bowder's dog has been quiet?" cried the poor old woman, raising herself on the couch, where she spent the greater part of the hours she did not pass in bed, and pointing to the extra pillow she was too fretful and disquieted to ask for.

She was a singular exception, Catherine Warren, to the rule among her kind, to the gentleness of temper and large-souled patience, the temperance of thought and tolerance of spirit that distinguish the ex- and the emergent Quaker. It may be that when she "left Friends," she had suffered from being cut adrift in a way that minds of better balance do not, and that her restless spirit, too intelligent for compromise, though too weak for independence, had not since found an anchorage. Add to this her nervous temperament and almost unremitting sufferings, and it will be understood that she was no light charge, even to her dutiful, robust, and placid sister.

It was with a slow and inelastic step, and with a very sad little face, that Stella left her aunt's room and sought the quiet of her own to hold such communings with her Muse as she could—her Muse, who had been clogged, and gagged, and paralyzed till she was dumb as Baal of old, till, clamour as her hungry votary might, there was neither voice, nor any to answer, nor any that regarded.

And this is where the "tone-poet" suffers

beyond his brother poets in colour, in marble, in language. He is the most dependent of all artists upon media of expression that are often costly, complicated, unwieldy; he is fain to lean more upon the skill of others, and, for that matter, often, too, upon the patience of others. Rob a painter of his colours, and he will console himself with the pencil; take pen and paper from the thinker, and he still has thought and memory. There are more materials than one upon which the plastic art may exercise itself; but the musician without an instrument is like a child without his mother, shivering, and starving, and helpless, and ill at ease, and refusing to be comforted. " Some of them were like music," wrote the young Chopin of the pictures in a Gallery. Imagine that temperament debarred from music !

Stella's room was strewn with musical compositions of all kinds, in various stages of incompleteness. Some of the simpler ones, it is true, were finished; as the song " *Nur wer die Sehnsucht*," a valse or two, some organ voluntaries. But there were weightier things on hand; there was a Fugue begun, and there were a few sheets of a Cantata, and there was a fragment of a Concerto! How were these things to advance with no piano, and with only a crude, self-taught knowledge of Harmony? Nothing but the passionate patience of genius could have kept this girl, resolved and pale and sad, bending over her manuscripts throughout the June morning; shutting the window sometimes that she might help herself by humming a passage; wrestling with memory for some dimly recollected phrase; longing and longing, and longing for the touch that would kindle her brain, and the sounds that would quicken her soul.

Presently came a tap at the door, and a message that Miss Sarah was out, and would Miss Marryot speak to Mrs. Thomson?

" In a minute—in one minute," Stella said. She was in the middle of a bar, and the temptation to finish it was irresistible. Before she had put down her pen there was another tap, and Mrs. Thomson, a buxom banker's widow, had invaded the untidy sanctum, with its litter of blotted music-paper and books about music, its mementos of school-days, its penetralia of all kinds.

" I won't disturb you for more than two minutes, dear," said the bustling lady, who, since the death of the rector's wife, had been the head-clergywoman of Astlett. "I knew my way up, and I thought it would save you

coming down." And she settled herself into a
chair for half an hour's gossip. "I want you to
tell your aunt that I've found out the truth
about Marten, and that he really does *not* drink,
poor man! and it's all his wife, and he's getting
worse, and I want to consult with her as to the
best way of helping him. Then the Zenana is
put off—will you tell her?—till this day week.
Savin, stupidly, has not been able to get that
stuff. I wanted to save her the trot over to me.
Why, how busy you are, to be sure! What is
it all about?" And Mrs. Thomson laughed,
and took up the paper nearest to her with the
sans gêne indispensable to a clergywoman.

"Oh, that's only a little song I—I tried to
write," said Stella, crimsoning.

"What, do you write songs? You ought to
publish them," said Mrs. Thomson in a breath,
as though it were a *sequitur*. "Have you ever
tried?"

"Yes; once I did," said Stella.

"Well, and what did they say?"

"They said the songs were very—graceful, I
think they said; but, then, it cost far too much."

"But they ought to undertake them," said
Mrs. Thomson. "There's my cousin—I don't
exactly know how she managed, but, you know,
she made a hundred pounds nearly by her

things.   You know her things, the ' *Trout
Beck*,' and that ' *Show me the eyes.*'   Now,
look here, I'll tell you what I'll do.   I'll send
her some of your things, and get her to write
to her publishers for you, shall I ?   Why, this is
all waste of time unless you publish, isn't it ? "
And Mrs. Thomson looked cheerfully round
upon Stella's litter, as though she were not
sounding a funeral dirge over a thousand
strangled hopes.

But Stella's eyes had brightened at the unexpected, delightful offer.   She had often thought
of Mrs. Thomson's cousin as a possible helper ;
but, as usual, she had not had the courage to
take the initiative in the matter.   How could
she know that her compositions were worth one
of Mrs. Thomson's postage stamps?   All she knew
was that they were the life of her own soul.

She made a little packet of the ones she
thought most likely to win favour—the German
song, and a couple of English ballads ; her
hand shook a little as she twisted the paper
round them and put them, with a grateful
smile, into Mrs. Thomson's hand.

" I must try and get on with my Harmony,"
she said, hopeful all of a sudden, inspirited and
encouraged.

" Didn't you say Bolton was to teach you ? "

asked Mrs. Thomson. (Bolton was the schoolmaster and organist.) "Poor Bolton! I don't
know what's to be done, now he'll have to give
up the organ. Miss Savin's the only person
who can play it; but Mr. Marshall will never
give it to *her*."

"But is Bolton worse? Has he come back?"
asked Stella, excitedly.

"Come back, my dear, yes; but only to die,"
said Mrs. Thomson. "Didn't you know? Oh,
he's in galloping consumption; and Mr. Marshall has been advertising for a new master
already. It is so touching. I never saw such
a wreck. Poor Mr. Marshall and his organ!
It's a dilemma, isn't it? He won't hear of a
salaried organist, of course. I suppose we shall
go on being martyred by Miss Stock."

"If—— " said Stella, quickly, drawing herself
up in her chair, with a great light shining in
her eyes; "If Mr. Marshall would make *me*
organist, I would work for him night and day!"

Mrs. Thomson looked at Stella. Then she
laughed.

"*You?* Why, you little thing, you wouldn't
be strong enough," she said. "But I must be off.
Good-bye, dear, good-bye, and remember my
messages."

"Stella!" screamed Aunt Catherine, as the

girl was running upstairs, after seeing Mrs. Thomson out. With a weary sigh she turned aside into her aunt's room.

"Who was that, Stella? Who was that talking so loud and banging the doors? Mrs. Thomson, was it? Well, that'll do, you needn't stay. I just wanted to know who it was banging all the doors."

And so Stella, after waiting a moment uneasily, watching the querulous invalid writhe among her cushions, letting off steam in two or three ways at once, muttered the oft—oft repeated "I'm very sorry," and slipped back again to her room.

That dear little room!—with its pink-and-white hangings, its cosy old-fashioned bed, its quaint handsome furniture, its open windows shrouded in jessamine, through which she could see, beyond a beautiful garden and a green paddock, only a gently rising upland thickly studded with trees. Truly it is not in deserts alone, it is sometimes by the side of the cool-flowing rivers of glorious Babylon, and under the sweet, dark shade of her willows, that the heart of the exile is wasted.

Stella paused a moment, pen in hand, to think over what had happened. Her songs were in a fair way to receive the attention she

had found it impossible to claim for them
unaided—that was good. But how was she to
work on in the meanwhile? She had been
counting on the schoolmaster's return for pur-
suing her studies in Harmony, and so preparing
herself for the day which must come soon—
how should it not come?—when she should
have free access to some instrument. Bolton
was an intelligent man, and not unmusical.
He knew of her wish, and had for some months
past been refreshing his, at one time considerable, acquaintance with the science of music on
her account. But his health had been failing
for a long while; a protracted holiday appeared
to have accelerated instead of mitigated the
complaint. He had come home to die.

There was no one else in Astlett who understood Thorough Bass, or, indeed, who really
cared about music.

Stay, there was one person. The youngest
partner in the firm of Head Brothers was a
man of considerable culture, and of an acute
and versatile mind. He had lived on the Continent for some years; German, especially, he
spoke with great fluency, and read with keen
delight; he had a ready pencil, and was skilled in
clever caricature; his talk sparkled with lively
wit and satire, without ever being ill-natured;

he had a good tenor voice, and sang with what is better than " taste," and includes " taste " with feeling. He had been the first person in Astlett to find out Stella's gift. When she came home for the holidays, a sensitive school-girl of sixteen, shy with most people, singularly expansive and animated with any one who discovered the thoughtful, ardent, earnest woman in her, Gurney Head had drawn her out; had encouraged her singing in public—that is, in the Astlett drawing-rooms, and at the meetings of the Musical Society he had started; had often sang with her, and had given her many a light that was wholly outside the orbit of any of her school teachers, that confirmed her own intuitions, and sanctioned while it guided her own impulse.

And to say this much is to say a great deal more in the case of a young, gifted creature, as diffident as she was original in mind, and as modest as she was ambitious. Stella imagined that she owed a boundless debt of gratitude to her mentor of those dawning, doubtful, wistful years. How could she forget the way he distinguished her, when other people were treating her like a child, and helped and led her on; he, the thirty-years-old Alcibiades of Astlett, who had seen the Vienna and Venice operas, been at

Dresden concerts without end, and at more than one Wagner Festival? His bright smile may have gone for something—a peculiarly frank, luminous smile—that never lit up his quick brown eyes as it did when his *protégée* rendered, with the perfectness of passionate feeling, a song he loved, or played him a new composition that hit his fancy. There was a fascinating ease of manner about him, too—a warm natural way of talking, that had a great charm. When Stella had done singing or playing, he would seize her hands and say, " Thank you, oh, thank you, dear," like an elder brother.

An intimacy had existed for years between the Head family, which was numerously represented in and about Astlett, and the Warrens, their predecessors, with whom, indeed, they were connected by other than business ties.

Nobody in Astlett would be astonished to hear one of the Heads call Stella Marryot " dear."

Gurney was oftener absent than any of the partners ; and Stella, at this time, was seldom at home. When they did meet there was always this frank, pleasant, musical intercourse, the kind of thing that even in a gossiping country town excites no comment.

Once, indeed—it was years ago now, two

whole years—on a certain July evening, when there had been music at old Mrs. Head's, and a little surreptitious dancing, and open windows out into the moonlit garden, Stella could remember something happening that was not brotherly; something very trivial, probably— just the lowering of a voice, the momentary prolonging of a touch, some magic accentuation of the insignificant syllable " *you.*"

That was two years ago.

III.

THE Miss Warrens held, very naturally, the most rigid form of the domestic theory about women. They not only required, as it is to be trusted all good women ever will, that a girl should be a good housewife; they demanded—a somewhat unusual and to many an inconceivable demand in this ninth decade of a hurrying century—that she should be nothing else. Mrs. Fry, had they brought her up, would have been taught that prison reform was men's business; Mrs. Hannah More would have been grudged an hour stolen from samplers and preserving for the pen. And when it came to the desire of a girl's heart being set,

not upon philanthropy, but upon art, that is
upon a merely ornamental and egotistical pursuit, the offence was greater. It became needful
to take constant opportunities of checking the
irregular instincts—not, oh, not from any spirit
of persecution—of opposition even—but from
piety and principle, and the blinding force of
inherited temperament and traditions.

It really was not so much because Miss Sarah
wanted the strawberries picked as because she
did not want Stella to pass an " idle " afternoon,
that she sent her out into the kitchen garden
on one of these hot June days, just as Stella had
done composing, and was about to transfer to
paper a petition to Mr. Marshall for the post of
organist. It would have been impossible to make
the audacious request in person ; but Stella could
wax valiant on paper, like most of us ; and if
she was refused—why, it was but one sorrow
more. Her head was full of this letter as she
went out, armed with a milkpan and a little
stool, accompanied by Elizabeth and Jane with
more dishes and stools, and set to work upon
the strawberry-beds. The sun beat fiercely
down upon the clusters of ripe fruit, cushioned
upon hay and well covered with netting. All
was still save for the lowing of a cow in the
meadow, lately parted from her calf, and for the

thrushes' chatter. At a safe distance, eyeing the
women-kind, stood Robert, groom and gardener,
a personage who was always wanting help—
except when he got it.

At length came another sound—Stella's cough.

"There's that cough again!" said Elizabeth,
who had been Stella's nurse before she became
parlour-maid. "I do wish you'd take more care
of it. You know what your poor pa died of.
I'm always telling you you shouldn't run out
late of an evening with nothing on. Settin' up
so late, too, over them music things——"

"Don't scold, Lizze, I mean to be a very good
girl," said Stella, smiling; then, bending over
her work, and letting her voice drop, she added,
smiling still,—"I don't fancy, somehow, that I
shall die of a cough."

The next silence was broken by a distant
murmur of women's voices, and Aunt Sarah
presently appeared with a tall grey-haired lady,
soberly and simply attired in a compromise
between the old Quaker garb and modern dress;
sweet-voiced, and made beautiful, even in old
age, by her peculiarly brilliant eye.

Stella sprang to her feet, with a happy flush
suffusing her face. If there was one person in
Astlett from whom she would have joyfully
quitted a more absorbing pursuit than straw-

berry picking—had it been music itself—that person was Mrs. Head.

Women of advanced age have a way of thinking themselves uninteresting that is often curiously mistaken. They do not seem to know that they can inspire in young girls of ardent temperament feelings of the most romantic tenderness, the most enthusiastic devotion; they put the young love aside with some playful talk about "an old woman like me;" they will not always "inflict" their kisses on the lips that would be proud to touch their hands.

Stella had, all unknown to its object, such a girlish veneration for the bright-eyed and sweet-voiced widow, Mrs. Head.

This lady was Gurney Head's mother.

"Stella, we've come to tell you some news," said Aunt Sarah, as Stella held up a pair of juice-stained hands to show that to-day, at any rate, there could be no mode of greeting but a kiss.

It was a warmer one than usual that she got; there was such a flutter of maternal feeling in the widow's heart. But though they both looked so glad, Stella's heart had stopped beating before her aunt had finished her sentence.

Before they told her the news, before Mrs. Head spoke at all, she had felt the stab, and understood that life's highest joy had vanished from her life for ever.

" Yes, indeed it is true, my dear boy has lost his heart at last," said the old lady in musical tones, as she beamed her joy upon Stella ; "and to one who seems in every way worthy of him. A stranger to us all in Astlett, my dear; but I think Astlett will make her welcome. She is musical too, Stella! Very musical. We shall all think that a gain, shan't we ? "

" Oh, the greatest gain," Stella said, smiling, but in such a curious loud voice.

Then Miss Sarah told her who the lady was —a very pretty and fascinating person, whom Gurney had met at the Lakes—quite a chance meeting—the daughter of a colonel in the army, *i.e.* of a personage, from the Astlett point of view. It was altogether a most distinguished and auspicious affair. Miss Sarah was quite excited about it, and before night half the town was in a state of pleased agitation over the event. The Factory workpeople, with whom Mr. Gurney, the leader of their sports on holidays, the promoter of all schemes for their welfare and entertainment, the joyous, genial sympathizer and friend, was a prime favourite, set on foot a subscription for a silver ink-stand; the townspeople projected a triumphal arch, and resolved to take the horses out of the bride and bridegroom's carriage (they were not to appear in Astlett till after the wedding, as the lady's home was distant) ; the partners, while they felicitated each other on the young man being settled in life, made good-humoured arrangements for a liberal honeymoon ; the ladies of the place, headed by some members of the Musical Society, entered so heartily into the general jubilation as to talk about a bracelet— a very substantial proof of satisfaction in the marriage of a gentleman acquaintance—to somebody else.

"I'm very, very sorry I can't go back to the gate with you," Stella said, still in that odd, high-pitched voice to Mrs. Head, who was hurrying off to another house with her news ; "but the cook says she *must* have them by four o'clock!" And she laughed aloud, and made a dive down into the strawberry beds.

"Here's a monster!" said Elizabeth.

"It *is* hot," said Jane.

"There's four!" said Elizabeth.

"There's the front door!" said Jane.

"It's only Miss Marshall," said Elizabeth, stooping down again.

Dolly Marshall knew her way about, and had soon tracked Stella to the kitchen garden.

"Come over to St. Julyans with me, will you, Stella?" she shouted. "I've got a message to take for father, and nobody to go with!"

"All right," said Stella. She dared not plead a headache—not for fear of being found out, but for fear of waxing selfish in her grief.

She soon discovered to her unspeakable relief that Dolly had not heard the news. That made the drive easier to bear—the being whirled along in a two-wheeled pony-cart by a light-hearted girl for half a dozen miles. The road to the county town was not beautiful, except little bits here and there. The vale broadened out by degrees into a rather monotonous plain; you could not see much beyond tall hedges and telegraph posts. Such drives, unenlivened by genial companionships, are tedious at the best. To-day, to Stella, seated by the side of a cheery, healthy-minded girl, all life, all kindness—every tramp of the pony's hoof seemed to leave a mark on her heart.

When she got home, there was no time to be alone, and even after tea there was no time. Aunt Catherine was better; she had come downstairs, and wished to be read to. She never let Sarah read to her, if Stella was to be had, showing therein considerable discrimination; for Miss Sarah's voice was harsh and untuneable, and Stella's had the natural sweetness of the "singing throat," with that added strain of melody that is strangely lent to human speech by sadness.

What Stella read to Aunt Catherine was never in anywise interesting to herself; not that Miss Warren never read good books, but that she had a trick of selecting dry things when reading aloud was in question. It seemed almost like malice—but it was only irritability. And, then, Stella was not literary. The *Spectator* and the *Rambler* had hardly more interest for her than Low Church newspapers. Only a loving-hearted girl, with a sense of duty, be she artist or no, cannot say, "If you will kindly excuse me, I had rather not read to-night."

Bed-time came at last. At last—at last, came the luxury—not of help, not of sympathy, not of consolation—but of liberty to weep.

"Don't sit up, Stella dear," said Aunt Sarah, prophetically, as she bade her good-night. "Now, promise me you won't sit up."

"I promise I won't be very late, auntie."

"But I don't wish you to be at all late," said Aunt Sarah, with a trace of asperity in her tone. "I cannot have this perpetual sitting up, burning so many candles, besides the injury to health. Now, promise me you won't do it to-night."

"Very well, I won't," murmured Stella, as she turned aside to her room.

"By-the-by, did you hear, Bolton's gone?" said Aunt Sarah, turning round abruptly, and shading her candle.

For some reason or other, perhaps from the suddenness of the remark, Stella turned white, and gave a loud quick gasp.

"What's the matter, child? Bolton—only Bolton—I say, poor Bolton died this afternoon. Did I startle you? You knew he was dying. I must go and see the poor widow." And with that Miss Sarah turned a corner and disappeared.

And Stella shut the door of her little room, looked round upon her scattered treasures, took up and kissed one comely, fairly written sheet; then fell upon her bed and sobbed.

And from that soft and fragrant resting-place there went up once again that night the exceeding bitter cry which has been wrung from every woman-artist since time began—

"Oh Art, my Art, thou art much, but Love is more."

IV.

A CONSIDERABLE time elapsed before Mr. Marshall answered a note he received one day by the post from Miss Marryot, praying to be allowed to undertake the duties of organist in the room of Mr. Bolton. Possibly he was a long time making up his mind, forgetting— how should a Mr. Marshall remember?—that what is only indecision to authority is often slow torture to necessity; probably he had a dozen more pressing claims on his attention. He met Stella several times in the interval and talked of weather. At length, one day, she received a polite letter expressing sincere gratitude for her very kind proposal, but stating, that for various reasons, there would be no alteration of existing arrangements at present.

"I tell him he ought to have asked you," said the solicitor's wife, Mrs. Mahaffey, a talkative Irishwoman, who came to the working parties, and was much patronized by the *élite* of Astlett. "What did ye think of it last Sunday, eh? Didn't ye have to stop your ears, Miss Marryot? And to think of you having to sit

listening, and you longing to be at it yourself!
Weren't you?"

"I don't know why he wouldn't have me,"
said Stella, folding up her work. "I know Miss
Stock would be glad to give it up."

"Why, love, it's because you're half her
size; that's why it is," said Mrs. Mahaffey,
consolingly. "He don't believe you could
manage that great big organ; and I'm sure, to
look at you, nobody else would, with your
pretty white face and those mites of thin fingers.
Still, we all agree that to have the nice
hymns and things murthered by that great
bouncing Miss Stock is really beyond endurance."

"And did you—were you really kind enough
to say a word for me?" put in Stella, as they
left Mrs. Head's together.

"'Deed and I did, love, and before I knew
you had asked him, too. It was one day he
looked in to see Philip on business, and he began
admiring our new piano. 'Beautiful instrument,
to be sure, Mrs. Mahaffey!' You know the
sort of blarney, don't ye, dear?" And the
good lady paused a minute to laugh heartily at
her successful impersonation of the correct and
courtly rector. "But oh, you should have
seen his face when I said, 'And when are we

to have a new organist, Mr. Marshall?' I don't mind what I say to him, you know! I said, 'If you could get Miss Marryot, now,' I said, 'that would be a good job.'"

"And what did he say?"

"Oh, he hummed and hawed and looked as if I'd offered him a dose of physic, and then said something about 'no changes—no changes,' and Miss Stock doing very well; and he'd have been out of the house like a mouse out of a trap if I hadn't stood in the doorway and pretended not to see what he was at. 'You know,' I said, 'if there *is* a musical genius in the place,' I said, 'it's Miss Marryot.' And he couldn't deny that, but he said you were too young and not strong enough. He said perhaps in another year or two it might be arranged."

"Did he say that?"

"He said that; but he made such a face over it I had to let him go, for fear he'd have a fit."

"*Young!*" repeated Stella, stupified. She felt so very far from young in suffering.

"Well, and so you are young, love," laughed Mrs. Mahaffey, as she stopped at her own door. "There can't be two opinions about *that!* Miss Stock's a nuisance, but I'm not half sorry he wouldn't have *you*, for you'd have overdone it, I'll be bound, and made yourself ill looking after those rampaging boys. You just try and keep a choir of boys together!"

Whereupon Mrs. Mahaffey waved her hand and vanished.

She was a kind soul, whose vulgarity was tolerated on account of her good nature and benevolence. Astlett society, which was mainly composed of philanthropic semi-Quakers, looked on her as a valuable ally; whereas in circles untempered by such genial influences, she might very easily have become the victim of local satire, and been snubbed into unprofitable if not into mischievous activity.

The ten minutes' chat that wound up the Astlett working-parties had chanced to turn upon the death of Mr. Bolton that morning. Mrs. Thomson, who walked, as she did everything, energetically, and had caught up Stella soon after she parted with Mrs. Mahaffey, was still full of it. So were Rose and Edith Harrison, the doctor's daughters, who were almost as fond of "parish" as of lawn-tennis, and were great friends with Mrs. Thomson. These young ladies had been to a good school, dressed well, and were very quiet and unassuming; their only fault was that they were terribly young lady-like.

" You don't mean to say *you* really wished to be organist, Miss Marryot! " said the eldest, opening her mild blue eyes in unfeigned astonishment.

" That's what Mrs. Mahaffey told us! " echoed her younger sister, incredulously.

Little Stella began to feel that she had done something very " strong-minded," if not actually wicked. Was she very presumptuous, very misguided, to dream of any other life save theirs—their life of " parish " and lawn-tennis and art-needle-work ?

The buzzing talk about the organ made her so sick that she mustered courage to plunge into the subject which she knew was more absorbing to them than any other—lawn-tennis—and thus she let herself in for a pressing invitation to spend the afternoon with them over the magnificent game which has given a new zest to the lives of country girls, and promises to add a large percentage to the national stock of vigour, health, and spirits. She had no engagement to plead—nothing but the occupations which were ignored of all and disallowed of some, which were so overlooked and so contemned, and, by a strangely perverse fate, so hampered, impeded, and annulled, that a stouter heart might well have doubted whether they were, in the grand old Hebrew phrase, "of God," and a braver spirit might, in despair, have abandoned them and life together.

After the Harrison girls had turned down the lane that led to their house, Mrs. Thomson harked back to the Bolton family. One of the boys was to be got into the Bluecoat School; a situation as governess must be found for the eldest girl; how bread-and-butter was to be procured for the remaining children and for the widow was a problem, but people were subscribing liberally to the fund, and that would give breathing-time.

" Tell Aunt Sarah I'm coming to dun her for her ten guineas," wound up Mrs. Thomson, as she bade Stella good-bye.

While she was still holding her hand, something in the girl's face touched the kind woman.

" Stella, you must come to the seaside with me. I'm going to take my sister's children from St. Julyans there next week. I don't think this air suits you. How's the cough ?"

The cough was better, Stella said. Very few of us answer that kind of question truthfully.

" Well, you must just come with me to shake off the remains of it. I'll talk to your aunt about it."

And Mrs. Thomson was hurrying in, when

Stella said, hesitatingly, in the midst of her thanks, "Oh, Mrs. Thomson, in case—as you're going away soon—in case there is not another opportunity, did your cousin say anything about those songs?"

"Oh, to be sure! Why, fancy my forgetting all about it! I heard from her some days ago, saying she was going abroad for six weeks, next day, and couldn't possibly attend to them till she came back; but she'd have them returned to you, if you wished it."

"Oh, not if she's kind enough to look at them when she comes home!" said Stella, as brightly as she could.

"Oh, she'll do that with pleasure, I'm sure!" said Mrs. Thomson, encouragingly. "Very well, then, they'll *stand over.*" (Like a Zenana meeting, or Mrs. Bolton's future.)

It was not quite dinner-time, and something Mrs. Thomson said about the Boltons led Stella to stop at a cottage door very near her own gate. She had been too much neglecting her own poorer friends; she stood in great and increasing danger of growing sour and selfish in her grief.

The cottage was very lovely in its poverty. The walls and roof were covered with roses and traveller's-joy. On either side of the porch stood great clumps of hydrangeas. The blossoms had not quite settled what colour to adopt, but they were very luxuriant and plentiful. A wisteria from the next cottage stretched a gnarled bough half-way across this one, adding its quota of light green leaves to the wealth of colour there; a tree-fuchsia, too, leaned over the little party-wall, till its delicate crimson flowers almost kissed the pale hydrangeas. Within, there dwelt a fragile woman with sickly children, who had long been the object of Stella's special care, and to whom Miss Sarah sent frequent dinners, and many a little comfort, otherwise beyond her reach, though her husband was in receipt of good wages at the Factory. The good folk of Astlett knew how heavily chronic ill-health, as distinguished from acute illness, presses upon the industrious poor; how the diet that is wholesome, and the drudgery that is second nature in health, become nauseous and grievous to be borne, when the whole head is sick, and the whole heart faint; they entered tenderly into that constant cry for " nourishment," and felt what it imported; they gave freely from their own good tables good meat and drink to all the drooping ones.

It had often comforted Stella to go into the

cottages bearing some welcome gift or cheering message, and receiving love and blessings in return; and she never felt more hungry for that medicine than now, as she lifted the latch of the low door, having had no answer to her tap, and called, "Mrs. Andrews, may I come in?"

"Oh yes, come in, miss," said Mrs. Andrews, emerging from some back region, wiping her hands on her apron. But to-day she had no smile for Stella, and her answers were short. She was looking thinner and paler than ever, and her two poor arms, bare to the shoulder almost, were nothing but skin and bone, for all they had been so busy in the washtub.

Stella saw that something was wrong; and she took hold of the poor young creature's hand, now it was dry, and told her how very sorry she felt not to have been to see her for so long.

Then the storm that had been pent up with difficulty burst forth.

"It wasn't for her to speak, and she'd no right to say anything, and she couldn't say but what she'd had many a kindness from the Miss Warrens and Miss Marryot, and she hoped she wasn't ungrateful for all favours; still, she did feel being passed over. And she'd never had the milk but once, and then only for a short time;

and of course she didn't grudge it to nobody; but those that had good health and strong healthy children,—well, she hoped they knew how to be thankful for them; and nobody but them that had their children always ailing knew what it was, nor how thankful anybody is for a little help, such as a little good milk and such like."

And so the torrent of talk would have run on, if Stella had not stemmed it with a hurried promise that Mrs. Andrews should have some milk immediately, and made good her retreat on the plea of dinner. Mrs. Thomson, Mrs. Mahaffey, or Miss Harrison would have stayed to elucidate matters, and talk the woman into a good temper, but our poor little musician was too tender—too weak, perhaps—for such encounters. She could not do battle for her rights, even in a cottage. She could only grieve that in the midst of beauty—in a good and grateful heart, too—there should lurk what was so unlovely; she could only lament that strange vein of jealousy, suspicion, and petty graspingness which startles one at times among even the noblest of our poor.

At dinner she told her aunts about her visit. It was one of Aunt Catherine's " good " days— when she was able to come to early dinner, when every breath of summer air had to be shut out of the dining-room, and Elizabeth moved about warily with her dish-covers like a cat on ice.

"Complained of not having had the milk, did she, the ungrateful creature?" said Aunt Catherine, who had a quick eye for everything, especially other people's shortcomings. "Sarah, how you and Stella must have spoilt that woman!"

"Well, I have certainly done more for her than most," said Miss Sarah. "She's so young, and such an invalid!"

"Ah, but that spoiling process is a mistake," went on Miss Catherine. "Elizabeth, *how* often must I ask you to keep the door shut? If I could only get about! I think it's a sad mistake. Sarah, do you think the cook will ever learn that I can't eat thick toast? Elizabeth, do you think you could ask the cook for a slice or two of *thin* toast, or would it be asking *too* much?" And poor Miss Catherine's voice grew shriller and more shrill, till she almost cried over the offending toast-rack. "Take it away; that's it, take it away. My soup will be cold, but I can't help that. I can wait. What a singular thing, Sarah, that the cook shouldn't have learnt about the toast!"

" Are you going to drive to-day, Aunt Catherine?" asked Stella, who sometimes tried, though it was a thankless task, to give a pleasant turn to the talk at meals.

" Drive! How can I drive when I've had no dinner!" screamed Aunt Catherine, sitting disconsolate over her steaming soup plate. "What in the world is the good of talking about driving?"

" It's such a glorious day," Stella said.

" I'm glad you're going to spend the after-noon with the Harrisons," remarked Aunt Sarah, with a benign look. She had an uncon-scious way, the worthy soul, of approving whatever tried and wearied Stella most.

Stella knew so well what the topic of conver-sation would be that afternoon, and, had the game itself not overtasked her strength, would have shrunk from going to the Harrisons to hear a dozen indifferent tongues discuss the approaching reception of Mr. and Mrs. Gurney Head. She found them all—Rose and Edith, the Marshall girls, three young ladies from a neighbouring parsonage, and several Miss Heads—in the thick of it, and had to give her opinion about the arch, listen to detailed accounts of the new furniture that was ar-riving at old Mrs. Head's, who was to go on living, an honoured inmate, under her son's roof, and finally promise to subscribe to the bracelet.

"I'm sure *you'll* have more pleasure in subscribing than any of us," remarked Edith Harrison, innocently, "when you think what Mr. Gurney has done for the Musical Society."

"I wonder whether he'll get up the 'Elijah' now!" put in Kate Marshall.

"I hope Mr. Gurney will know our presents are for *him*," said her sister Agnes, gravely. "It's rather funny giving it to *her*, when it's meant as a thankoffering to him for all the pains he's taken about the Society."

"I half hope he will drop the 'Elijah' now," said Rose Harrison. "I know I never could take that solo."

"I think Gurney *bothers* too much," remarked one of Gurney's cousins. "Not one of us altos ever takes a wrong note, but he's down upon us in an instant. Do you remember the fuss he made the day Lizzy Savin had to take that contralto solo in 'St. Dorothea'—you know, '*O'er Cæsarea*,' instead of Stella?"

"Well, Miss Savin has no more voice than a cat," said another cousin.

"Well, but to make such a fuss about a trifle."

"Oh, well, I hated that 'Dorothea' altogether."

"I think he does choose rather stupid things." And so on, *ad libitum*.

V.

"I THINK it's very officious of Mrs. Thomson; that's what I think about it," said Catherine Warren, settling herself anew in the corner of the carriage. "As if we shouldn't be the first to see it if there was anything wrong with Stella! That woman must have her finger in everybody's pie. I'm very sorry indeed that you consented."

"Well, to tell you the truth, I have thought Stella looking poorly myself," said her sister. "I thought the change might be nice for her."

"Change! Now I should have thought you knew better than that, Sarah! What would my dear father and mother have said? How many 'changes' did we have when we were her age? I think of all follies of the present day that idea of having a 'change' as soon as your head or your little finger aches is the most preposterous. Dear me! If people were all such sufferers as I am! Those

Boltons now. As if the man couldn't have
made up his mind to die quietly at home! He
must needs have a ' change,' and went and got
a chill that carried him off. And that Mrs.
Savin! I believe she takes her children to the
seaside as regularly as possible, and will do till
they catch a fever in some of those lodging-
houses. What she can want—— "

" Have you noticed that cough of Stella's ? "
put in Miss Sarah.

" Cough ? Oh, to be sure she's had a little
cold, and summer colds *are* tiresome things.
I'm sure if you've promised the child the treat
I should be the last person to grudge it her.
It doesn't matter about *my* missing her company
and reading aloud—oh, dear no, of course not ;
it doesn't matter about *that*," whined poor Miss
Catherine in reproachful irony.

" Indeed, my dear sister, you know that it
does matter, and that I didn't consent without
weighing matters well," said the good Sarah ;
" but the truth is, now Mrs. Thomson has mentioned it, I do think her looking decidedly thin ;
and she's not left Astlett since she came home
from school a year ago."

" Have *I* left Astlett since she came home a
year ago ? " cried Miss Warren, in such an
exalted key that even Dobbin, who was used

to her, pricked his ears, and would have turned round to see what was going on if Robert had allowed him. "Have *you* left Astlett since she came home a year ago? If Stella is not satisfied with her home——"

"Stella is perfectly satisfied with her home," interrupted Miss Sarah, with a touch of impatience. "I must say she is a dear girl, a very good girl. Of course she is satisfied. What more could a girl want than she has?"

What, indeed!

It would be untrue to say that the thought of what she called Stella's "practising" did not cross Sarah Warren's mind then; but sister Catherine was naturally a little sensitive on that point—besides, it was but a trifle.

So it was settled that Stella was to go with Mrs. Thomson and her nephews and nieces to the seaside.

The prospect was not exactly an exhilarating one. Mrs. Thomson, though like almost everybody in Astlett, the soul of kindness, was perhaps the least fitted of them all to undertake the functions of Stella's nurse and caretaker. Hers was that very common form of kindness which is a total stranger to tenderness, and has little to do with sympathy; it was the redundance of an active and cheerful nature, the natural overflow of gregarious instincts, and a comfortable income. She was the most matter-of-fact of women, ignoring, as few people dare do—ignoring naïvely and naturally the mighty interests that sway mankind—science, politics, art, literature, and most of the nobler developments of religion. She never had time to read anything, even a newspaper. She was puzzled by enthusiasm. She did not know enough about imagination even to be afraid of it. She was, like most persons who live in the present, an incessant talker, and Stella trembled to think what it would be to be shut up in small lodgings with her, to say nothing of the riotous children whose mother, being an invalid, had never attempted to control them. Deprived as her companion would be of the routine occupations that filled up her bustling days at home, there would be nothing at the sea for her to do but work—and talk.

And yet Stella's first sensation on hearing that her aunts had arranged for her to go with Mrs. Thomson, almost without having consulted her in the matter, was one of inexpressible relief. It was the first week in August, and they were to be away a month; consequently they would not be present at the wedding festivities, which were to take place early in September.

To obtain so great a boon, Stella was willing to run the gauntlet of the lodgings, and the talk, and the children, and the absence of all possibility (in Astlett there was always the *possibility*) of musical enjoyment. She would put the best face on it she could. She would try and like one or two, at any rate, of the spoiled children ; she would listen all day long to the music of the sea ; she would secure a few quiet hours to finish the Fugue; she would take with her that small hoard that had *not* been spent on a guitar, and see whether, in a large place like that to which they were going, it would not procure her some lessons in Harmony.

Of a project like the last of these it was not natural to Stella to speak to any one. She had met with so much discouragement about everything concerned with her higher aims. The bitter lesson that our sublimest duties are too often a species of forbidden fruit—to be snatched, like illicit pleasures, from out the turmoil of daily life—had been so ground into her from childhood, that it had become a second nature to her to conceal these things.

One has seen animals—affectionate and faithful-hearted dogs—cower apologetically and hide away ashamed when they are rebuffed or trodden on—as though the fault were theirs.

In this case, however, it was tolerably certain that the Miss Warrens would not have refused to sanction Stella's scheme. She was at least exempt from the numbing sense that she was acting in opposition to their express wishes.

It happened, fortunately for her, that the first day at the seaside was cold and showery, so that Mrs. Thomson kept the children indoors, and she was free to go out by herself to make inquiries in the town about a master. She was slipping downstairs, as she hoped unobserved, when a cough which she could not entirely suppress caught Mrs. Thomson's quick ear.

The sitting-room door opened.

"Why, Stella, you're never going out this weather?"

"Oh, it's hardly raining at all now," Stella said. "I had a little thing to do in the town."

"Won't it keep till to-morrow? Oh yes, I'm sure it will. You know you're in my charge, and I'm not going to let you do anything imprudent. Talk of Devonsea being relaxing! Why, I'm sure it's as cold as January at Astlett. And the damp so bad for your cough, too. Do just come in and see our feast. Dora, have you got a cup of tea for Stella? There, come in and take your hat off. Seriously, I can't have you go out, Stella dear. Now, Guy, where's some bread-and-butter?"

" The stupid dolls have eaten it all," said Guy, who was outgrowing "pretence" repasts.

" Well, now, and what was the commission?" went on his aunt. " Couldn't Nurse do it?"

It was in vain that Stella tried to parry the question. She had to make a clean breast of it, and tell Mrs. Thomson about her quest.

Mrs. Thomson—a rare thing for her—reflected a minute or two.

"I remember, poor Bolton was to have taught you," she said. " Did I ever tell you I've got as good as a promise from Alderman Davies for a presentation for Georgie? I worked pretty hard for it, I can tell you. I suppose it *would* be some use—Thorough Bass: we didn't learn it at school. Well, we'll see about it to-morrow, if it's a fine day."

Mrs. Thomson was so determined, that Stella could not have insisted further without being ungracious. She was receiving kindness at her hands; she was bound to defer to her wishes. In the morning——

But in the morning, when Stella had her things on ready to go out with the rest, and was standing on tip-toe to look at the sunlit sea, which she could just catch a glimpse of over the parapet in front of her attic window, Mrs. Thomson came in to dash her hopes.

"All ready, Stella dear? I just came to say that I've been thinking over what you told me about the Thorough Bass, and I've come to the conclusion that it would be *very much* wiser for you not to think of anything of the kind. You're not strong, and you've come here for health and a thorough holiday, and, in my opinion, you should do nothing at all but simply enjoy yourself with me and the children. I feel sure that would be your aunts' wish; and, for my own part, I'm not at all sure that I approve of young ladies keeping up their studies after they've left school." Here Mrs. Thomson chuckled good-humouredly. "We must shake you up a bit; that's what we must do. Come out on to the beach. It's so glorious out, only there's a cold wind. Imagine Devonsea being so cold in August! Now, don't think me a cross old woman, will you?" added the good lady, who did not dream of any revolt against her authority, or even understand that she was requiring a sacrifice.

Now it is possible to be very old at nineteen— to lay the plans that will one day revolutionize kingdoms, and dream the dreams that quickly

take immortal shape and live as joys for ever;
but it is also possible to be very young at
nineteen; to have qualms about a private in-
terpretation of duty; to be very fearful of
sacrificing love—the minutest fraction of the
tepidest love—to ambition; to be very careful
of calling disobedience strength, and obstinacy
firmness.

And Stella let her friend slip her arm
through hers and lead her downstairs. Mrs.
Thomson was chattering on, hardly waiting
for the assent which she took for granted,
when she was startled by feeling a nervous
pressure on her arm.

"Oh, do you hear them?"

"Who—the children?" cried Mrs. Thomson,
alarmed.

"No; that band."

"Oh, the band! What of that?" said Mrs.
Thomson, proceeding placidly downstairs.

But Stella, all whose nerves were tingling,
made a rush at the door to run on and get out
of earshot of the horrible din which hurt her
all the more because the tune they were playing
was her favourite Volkslied, "*Es zogen drei
Bursche wohl über den Rhein*," and because
every time they repeated the plaintive burden,
the hideous discord of the jangling instruments

seemed to burlesque the words that were graven
on her heart—

> "Dich liebt'ich immer, dich lieb'ich noch heut
> Und werde dich lieben in Ewigkeit."

She ran till she came to a great building,
the Devonsea Bath Saloon, which stood on the
cliff at the turning where the road led down to
the sea. She paused before a window, where
a flaring placard announced that several well-
known vocalists would appear at a concert to
be given the following week; and her heart
swelled with gladness as she reflected that there
was nothing to prevent her hearing them.

To hear music! It was bliss she had not
dreamed of, for she had never been to a large
watering-place in August before, and she knew
little of the ways of such places. She had—it
is almost difficult to write it as one thinks of
what it imports—she had only been to three
concerts in her life—in the winter-time at St.
Julyans—at intervals of about a year. The
passers-by, who had come to Devonsea for the
sixth or seventh time, and avoided musical and
other entertainments out of London, would have
wondered to be told that the girl, standing so
still and looking so hard at those red and blue
letters, was weeping for joy.

" I say, Stella, do come down to the beach and help me to build a castle for the little ones!" said Guy, suddenly pulling her gown. " Come on, let's get there before auntie ! "

But Stella did not answer him, for her eye had been caught by an unpretending little bill in writing near the large one. It announced that the piano within was at the disposal of the public in the day-time on payment of a shilling an hour.

" I say, Stella, do come on!" persisted Guy, who had been taught to look on grown-up people generally as his contemporaries.

" Come along," Stella said, cheerily, as she took him by the hand.

That was a happy—such a happy day for Stella! All the morning, while she built sand-castles, and told stories, and pulled shoes and stockings off and on, she was dreaming of the afternoon ; and all the afternoon—two hours of it, at any rate—she spent over the piano with the Fugue and a Trio for female voices beside her, and such an unaccustomed rush of fresh creative impulse and free, spontaneous pleasure as she had not known for many and many a day. She had never written before with so much care and pains ; but it was the care that is soul-absorbing, and the pains that are rapture. The very evening was happy. It was chilly, but it was clear and bright. A light wind ruffled the surface of the harbour, causing the slender spars of the yachts at anchor there to sway softly to and fro in the twilight. They were beginning to show their lights. Here and there you could see a dusky figure moving about on deck. On board one beautiful schooner, Stella could distinguish from her post in the balcony two girls in white wraps, pacing up and down with their father, each with an arm slipped through his. And as she sat brooding over the sweet scene a strain of perfect melody broke upon her ear, a voice from the open windows of the adjoining house singing with faultless purity of tone and accent Schumann's *"Ich grolle nicht."*

Would the voice stop when that was done? No; it went on; and Stella, with half-closed eyes, with all

    " The feverish joy, and dumb, delicious pain "

of such a moment, listened entranced to *"Er, der herrlichste von allen,"* and to the " First Violet " of Mendelssohn. " By Celia's Arbour " was begun when Mrs. Thomson came out on to the balcony.

" Do keep that shawl over your mouth, dear,"

she said; "I'm a little afraid of the night air for you."

" I'm *so* happy ! " Stella said.

" That's right ; I'm so glad. I think we *are* very happy together."

Mrs. Thomson lingered a moment to examine the weather.

" I think it's a shade milder than last night," she remarked.

Then a thrilling note from the musician next door drowned her voice.

"Ah, that's the worst of seaside lodgings——" she said ; " one's neighbour's piano."

VI.

STELLA had been at Devonsea about a week, when one afternoon, as she was lingering in the balcony, hoping for the sweet strains that were her daily solace, the singer herself, for the first time, stepped out of her drawing-room, gazing long and intently at the harbour, the smiling bay, and the dim outline of a distant headland. Stella, meantime, could, with impunity, gaze long and intently at her. She seemed to her not unworthy of the gift of her voice. She was a young-looking woman of thirty, one of the

few who combine, at that age, the contour and
freshness of girlhood with the repose and dignity
of maturity. She was dressed with the rare
taste which is independent of fashion, because
it can afford to be so ; her features, if not
strictly beautiful, were intensely prepossessing ;
and that she was a person of cultivated mind
was apparent from the nature of the open book
that she carried in her hand, a copy, as Stella
could see—she was so near her—of " Faust."
Only that was wanting to deepen the impression
the first sight of so much grace and charm made
upon Stella. Not that she knew much about
" Faust," but everything German was passion-
ately dear to her ; first, because Germany was
the home of music, and secondly, because she
associated it with the memory of her mother.
The German tongue had come to her with a
strange sort of familiarity at school; and with
any one who knew and loved it, she instantly
felt a mystic bond of sympathy. She was
falling deeply in love with the fair interpreter
of Mendelssohn and student of Goethe,
when her companion's voice recalled her to
herself.

" Come in here, Stella ! I've found out something so odd ! "

" What is that ? " said Stella, who had to pick

up a baby or two before she could get to Mrs. Thomson.

" Why, the lady next door is your relation, Lady Marryot! I had it just now," said Mrs. Thomson, who was struggling with another baby and a Visitors' List. "There it is. (Pier Terrace, No. 9, Lady Marryot and party.) That must be your Lady Marryot?"

" Yes; there is no other," Stella said, turning pale with surprise and excitement. "I know the baronetcy went to a cousin, quite a young man. My father had only that one brother, you know, who died very soon after succeeding to the title. How strange!"

" I do think that is the oddest coincidence! We really ought to make her acquaintance!"

" Oh no," said Stella. "They none of them know anything about me. I don't think they even know of my existence."

" Well, it's time they should," said Mrs. Thomson. " It seems to me an excellent opportunity for reminding them of it. It's not as if your poor, dear father had done anything to be ashamed of. They say he would have been quite a remarkable artist if he had lived; and as for his marriage—well, certainly your mother took more after her German relations than after the Warrens; but after all, *her* mother was a

Warren, one of a most worthy, highly respectable——"

"I suppose being *respectable* goes for nothing among grand people?" interrupted Stella, gravely. Probably she was thinking of some things she had heard at school.

"I suppose that German connection was the thing," went on Mrs. Thomson. "Of course, you've often heard how it came about? You know your grandmother—she was, I should think, a dozen years older than your Aunt Catherine — was travelling on the continent, after the peace of 1815, with old Mr. Gurney Head and a party, and there fell in with your grandfather, who seems to have been a sort of a——"

There Mrs. Thomson paused in some embarrassment.

"Oh yes, I know," said Stella, simply. "He was a sort of adventurer."

"Yes; but so handsome and plausible he took them all in, Gurney Head and all, and ended by marrying the rich Miss Warren."

"And I suppose it was grief she died of soon afterwards?" said Stella.

"No doubt about it. And then, of course, her little girl, your mother, grew up among the Germans. A good thing her father didn't live

long after that. Sarah's often told me the
Warren's kept their eye upon her all along, but
the German relations wouldn't give her up. I
suppose they'd found out her voice, and thought
they could make money out of her."

" I wonder how she kept so sweet and good,
as I've always heard she was ! " said Stella.

" Ah, that was a wonder ! "

" I wonder if that's what my father liked in
her when he met her at Prague. I hope it
was," said Stella.

" Well, then he brought her to London, as
you know," went on Mrs. Thomson, " and she
gave up public singing. And your aunts
tracked her out, and gave you a welcome."

" But my father's people cast him off, or at
least held aloof from him," put in Stella.
" No," added the girl proudly, " I would not
have anything to say to them now, even if there
were any left near enough to know anything
about me."

But Mrs. Thomson was not quite so sure.
Cousins were cousins, and a baronet was a
baronet. She did not feel at all clear that it
was not her duty to introduce Stella to Lady
Marryot, now that a coincidence almost amounting to providential interposition had brought
them together. She had serious thoughts of

calling on her neighbour next day; and all
Stella's entreaties would probably have failed to
divert her from her purpose, had she not fortunately remembered that she had promised the
elder children an excursion to Breezy Head, if
the morning were fine.

Stella was relieved to see the sun shining
brightly when she rose betimes, to be ready for
the early train. She felt the strangest mixture
of longing and repugnance towards her lovely
and accomplished cousin, and was thankful to
feel that she was to spend the live-long day
away from the town, out of reach of the resistless fascination of her siren voice.

She was seated in the train, helping Mrs.
Thomson to check the exuberance of Guy and
Dora, who were already contemplating a raid
on the luncheon-basket, when the door was flung
open again, and a porter, just in time, thrust
Lady Marryot, a governess, and three little girls
into the carriage.

Mrs. Thomson gave Stella a look that said
plainly, " You see, *it is to be*;" and, with
dogged resolve and a great air of dignity,
barely allowing Lady Marryot time to compose
herself in her seat, opened the attack.

"Lady Marryot, I think?"

Lady Marryot inclined her head courteously.

She seemed so gentle and genial, and had such an air of infantine sweetness and simplicity about her, that in that instant the longing conquered the repugnance in Stella's heart; and as Mrs. Thomson went on to talk about the cousinship, and the coincidence, and the musical sympathies, and what not, she herself put out her hand to her with a flush of pleasure. Lady Marryot was very pleased to make her acquaintance, and hoped they would be able to have some music together. She found the evenings long, Sir Henry being away in Scotland, shooting. She would like very much to hear Miss Marryot play and sing.

She seemed, by the way she talked, to know something about Stella's parentage, and she mentioned Claude Marryot, the father, with the familiarity of a relative, and with the pitying respect due to genius cut off in its prime. She gave one the idea of a person thoroughly unworldly, a person deeply, not superficially, interested in art, and genuinely preferring culture in all its forms to frivolity. She began to question Stella—while Mrs. Thomson, expressly to facilitate a *tête-à-tête*, chattered with the children and their governess—in a way that implied a strong individual interest in her—as though she were seeking to fathom her character, and concerned to know the details of her history.

Stella had never been questioned so, or had such a pair of expressive grey-blue eyes, veiled with long dark lashes, turned upon her in kindly scrutiny, reading her through and through—so it seemed to her—but all to soothe and sympathize and do her good.

" You ought to have a contralto," said Lady Marryot, smiling.

" So I have," said Stella ; " but how can you tell ? "

"Oh, one gets to know. I know so many musical people."

" I wish I did," Stella said.

" But you must know some—so fond of it as you are. And you compose, too, your friend says. You must know some musical people ? "

" No ; not one, not one," said Stella, hurriedly, her colour heightening. " One of the girls at school and one person in Astlett *loved* music— that's all."

The gaze of quiet scrutiny became more intent, but at the same time a shade, just a shade, less sympathetic. For the small, pale girl was quivering with emotion more unaccountable than interesting. What could there be in the conversation to make even a musical genius change colour, and work her hands restlessly, and try to hide by an attempt at a smile the patent fact that her eyes were filling ?

"If you will come home with me after the concert, I will introduce you to a musical person !" said Lady Marryot, gently. "You know Fidelia is to sing? She is one of my greatest friends, and has promised to come in to supper with me. She has practically retired, but consented to sing to-morrow, on account of a strong personal interest in the Asylum. She is a charming woman, and talks as well as she sings. I hope you will come."

It is needless to say with what effusive gratitude Stella assented to her cousin's proposal. She would have liked to stoop and kiss the hand that held her own so caressingly and long when they parted at the Breezy Head Station. It was so wonderful to have found a friend at last— some one all sympathy, all mind—all refinement ; some one she could love at first sight ; and who seemed to love her at first sight for her own and for music's sake.

But it chanced that the evening of that summer holiday was wet ; that a deluge of rain, wholly unexpected, drenched the little party, children and all, to the skin ; that they came

home crestfallen, and anxious as to the conse-
quences of the adventure; and that the one of
them all who was the least fitted to endure
illness was the only one who took any harm
at all.

Struck with a sudden chill of an alarming
character, Stella coughed all through the night,
and in the morning she herself was fain' to
own she was too ill to leave her bed. All day
long she lay there, tossing from side to side in
feverish misery; watching the sunlight—it was
all she could see through her attic window—
ripple among the magenta roses on the wall;
counting the magenta roses from the corner
nearest her, to where the sloping rafters inter-
cepted her view; listening to the wailing of
the poor teething baby in the adjoining room—
sometimes to two crying together; thinking of
her new-found friend, and of the joys that were
to have been hers that day.

"You will tell Lady Marryot I couldn't help
it?" she said to Mrs. Thomson once.

Towards afternoon some street acrobats came
noisily along the terrace. She could fancy
how the sun was shining on the spangled skirts,
on the discoloured drum, and on those screech-
ing panpipes. She wondered idly who there
could be to look on in the deserted houses; and

whether the old lady in the mushroom hat, who appeared to be the owner of the biggest yacht now lying alongside the pier, and who sat on deck all day long doing nothing, would come on shore to see them.

Towards evening came the sound of many carriage-wheels, rolling past on their way to the concert. Stella could hear them roll, then stop, then roll again; the Saloon was so near. She almost fancied later that she could hear Fidelia's glorious voice pouring forth the sacred sweetness of her heart in an aria of Handel, and then some one—a master—drawing the soul out of her own instrument, her piano—not the mediocre thing they let out to hire—a special one, perfect in touch and tone.

It was only fancy, of course. An artist's fancy must be vivid.

" Now don't listen to all these sounds any more, but try and go to sleep," Stella's good friend said to her, as she wished her " Good-night." " I want to get the mind quieter, or we shall have to call in the doctor to-morrow. You've just got a common cold on the top of your cough, and it will pass off naturally, if we could but get that restless little *mind* quiet."

Stella seized Mrs. Thomson's hand and held it in both hers. " If you *would* but go in and see Fidelia instead of me!" she cried with a terrible earnestness.

But it was dark, and Mrs. Thomson only thought her feverish and excited. "Why, Lady Marryot doesn't want *me*!" she said playfully. "Besides I don't fancy those sort of people much, you know. What would be the good of my going?"

"Only, then, I should have known to-night what she is like," Stella said.

Mrs. Thomson gave a sigh of mystified dissatisfaction as she left the wayward maiden's room.

VII.

"I DECLARE, Auntie, that Stella is a stupid thing!" remarked Master Guy, as he burst into the drawing-room, where Mrs. Thomson was sitting alone the first day that Stella came downstairs. "What do you think? We were playing at shops in the nursery, and we wanted some paper, and I knew she always had lots; so I went into her room, and she wasn't there, and I took some old sheets, all scribbled over with music and rubbish, and we tore them up; and when she came upstairs we asked her to come and buy, and she came and bought some

sweeties, wrapped up in the paper, of course—
real half-pennies she gave us—and then she
looked at the paper, and ran out of the room,
crying—oh! crying exactly like me or Dora
would! I don't think it *could* have been the
paper, do you? Don't you think it was very
stupid of her?"

"Oh, it couldn't have been *that!*" said Auntie,
re-assuringly. "Didn't you ask her?"

"No; I thought I'd come and tell you," said
Guy, who had a good deal of conscience for a
spoiled child, and always liked to have the blame
satisfactorily settled upon somebody else. "Oh,
she ran away into her own room, crying like
anything!"

"You see her bad cold has made her feel
weak and ill—that was it," remarked Mrs.
Thomson, placidly. "Now run off, Guy; I'm
busy writing to mother. Run away!"

Guy did not run, his thoughts were too busy,
but he walked away in complacent silence.

He had not, however, shut the door behind
him, when Lady Marryot was announced, and
he was bidden to run and tell Stella.

He found her sitting there by the little bare
table in the little bare room, while a fresh wind
—all too fresh for her—blew down on her from
the open window, stirring the disordered hair on

the pale forehead, and fanning those red spots on
either cheek that told—for Heaven forbid they
should tell any other tale!—of her passionate
weeping.

On her knees there lay the fragments—the
torn and crumpled fragments—of her Trio. Was
it gone for ever, the child of her brain's travail,
of her heart's love; the offspring of so many
tender dreams, so many hours of labour? Ah!
it might still linger—the substance of it—in
the soul; but, then, it had become so dear already
in its tangible shape! And how many and
many a weary day must pass ere it could be
re-written! It was a trouble to be very easily
borne, coming singly, and in health; very hard
to bear as one wave more upon a sea of
trouble—and in sickness.

Certainly trouble, like youth, is "a relative
thing." Take this girl Stella's circumstances,
for example. The modern definition of hell
is — the organism out of harmony with its
environment. To the seeing eye it would have
been plain that Stella's environment was slowly
killing her. To the Astlett folk it was, "What
more can a girl want?"

Even the thought that her gentle sympathetic
cousin had come to comfort her brought no
healing to the heavy-laden spirit. Wearily she

waited till the traces of her tears had faded, and wearily she moved down the steep narrow staircase, holding on to the banisters as though she had not strength to support herself, lingering on the landing-places as though to put off as long as possible the moment when she must smile.

Lady Marryot started back when she came in —the alteration in her was so marked—but she said nothing, only came forward and put her hands on her shoulders, and gave her a warm caressing kiss, that was full of tender meaning.

"You are my cousin, and I acknowledge you ; you are ill, and I pity you ; you are a musician, and I admire and honour and understand you."

All this and more was spoken by those soft lips in sweet lingering inarticulate language, and they brought the life back to Stella's soul, and sent the warm blood coursing in swift, glad pulsations through her veins.

For an hour or more they sat talking together, hand in hand, Evelyn Marryot, like an angel of consolation, cheering the drooping girl, whose mental history seemed as an open book to her, with whatever was best calculated to amuse and interest her, discussing German authors, relating her own musical experiences, giving her advice, and asking her for it, letting fall many an encouraging word, as it were casually, in her

varied talk. She told her several anecdotes of
Fidelia, and ended with the delightful announcement that she was to remain at Devonsea some
days. "So that you *will* see her after all!"

It was true the doctor had forbidden Stella to
go out, but Lady Marryot maintained that next
door was not "out." Stella should muffle herself in wraps, and come in and meet the great
personage at luncheon on Tuesday—four days
hence. She would be well enough then.

"I'm well enough *now!*" Stella said, in a
flush of excitement and gratitude, as her cousin
rose to go. She could not say all she would
before good Mrs. Thomson. She went downstairs with her new-found friend, and with that
strong dual enthusiasm of hers, the enthusiasm
of love, and the enthusiasm of genius, she seized
and kissed the succouring hand.

"Thank you for being so very kind to me,"
she murmured.

She lived upon the prospect of that glorious
Tuesday till it came, half-forgetting the forbidden
Harmony, the torn Trio, the piano that she was
not to be allowed to touch again; half-rejoicing
in her sleeplessness at nights, so enthralling
were her waking visions of the joy that was
before her.

Punctually at the appointed hour—an early

one, for the friends were to have some music together before Fidelia arrived—she entered her cousin's room. Lady Marryot threw down her book, and advanced with outstretched hands to meet her. Again, she did not say a single word, but, this time, in playful mood, led her straight to the piano, and laid her fingers on the keys.

"What am I to do?" asked Stella, half doubting, all enraptured, looking up into her sweet blue eyes.

"She doth not compose Symphonies as yet; her soaring spirit hath not yet aspired to write in score," quoth Evelyn, in merry girlish assumption of the sibylline vein (Stella had kept the Cantata secret); "but in 'one-hearted themes for one-voiced instruments' she hath no peer! Sweetly can she make and play them, and ere long the halls of St. James and Albert shall echo with her praise!"

Then Stella laughed aloud for joy, and, entering with all her heart into the sport, expressed her gladness in one of her own valses—the most inspired and impassioned of them all. Half-memories of Chopin floated through its refined and tender harmonies, like the whisper of the winds among undulating tree-boughs. It was imitative in part, as works of genius are at first—have a right to be always, Goethe says.

But it had the ring of the true metal, as Lady Marryott saw, as she had divined that Stella's work would have, the first time she looked into her eyes; and, yielding to an irresistible impulse, she went and laid her hands on the girl's shoulders as she finished, and said——

"You must play that to Lord Holbrooke!"

"Lord Holbrooke!" repeated Stella, bewildered.

Lady Marryot looked a little—a very little embarrassed.

"An uncle of my husband's who is coming to luncheon," she explained. "That would suit his taste exactly. He arrived last night in his steam-yacht, and sent word he was coming to luncheon. I am very sorry to say I have had to put off Fidelia in consequence. He would not care to meet her."

Probably Evelyn Marryot, accustomed as she was to the tepid emotions of "society," expected some polite, conventional rejoinder. If she did, she was disappointed. The blow to Stella was so severe, that she did not so much as try to collect her thoughts, but simply gazed at her cousin in mingled grief and amazement.

"*Not care to see Fidelia?*" she repeated at last.

Then Lady Marryot seemed to become

conscious of the wondering gaze of those innocent eyes, and she coloured deeply.

" Well, Lord Holbrooke is a little bit the old
school," she said, walking to the window, where
she stood, her tall straight figure outlined
against the light, with her hands clasped
behind her. " Fine manners, and ultra-
strictness, don't you know ? You can't dis-
regard their prejudices—you can't do it. He
is very fond of music—of *some* music ; but his
prejudice is against professionals."

" Then this is no place for me," thought
Stella, bitterly. " I am not so favoured as to be
able to '*profess*' my art. I can but worship
her as the Christians of old worshipped, trodden
underfoot of men, in the recesses of the Cata-
combs ; but I will not stay here to see her
spurned. If Fidelia is unworthy to meet him,
what must I be ? "

She turned to the piano in her confusion, as
Evelyn had turned to the window, and murmured, as she played with the music on the
desk, something about fearing that she should
be in the way, and not staying for luncheon.

" Come and see my photographs," said Lady
Marryot, affecting not to hear her—*not* hearing, probably, the bitterness in her tone.

She was all smiles when Stella sat down

beside her, with the big album on her knee; but her smiles had lost their magic—the whole bitter process of disillusion, often so protracted, had been completed the instant Stella found, that with all her sweetness, grace, and talent, she was not single-hearted.

Lady Marryot's book was full of great people—her husband's relations chiefly. Her own were represented in smaller numbers—a cynic might have argued because the family she came of, though "good," was not historic and not titled. Yet Evelyn had nothing of the vulgar tuft-hunter in her nature. She was born with a preference for rank, that was all, just as Stella was born with a predilection for music. She admired it, thought it beautiful, refined; associated it with governing intellect (as a sort of salve to her conscience), with statesmen unbending, and *attachés* paying sweet outlandish compliments; she had the *naïveté* to admit as much, to expect other people, whether they held her own views upon other subjects or no, at any rate to agree with her as to the inherent superiority of "a man who is a lord over a man who is not."

"You will like Lord Holbrooke," she said to Stella over the album, perhaps unconsciously seeking to win over this, the first heretic that she had met. "He is a very charming man! He was in diplomacy some years, and speaks French and Spanish and Italian and German perfectly. He mustn't see I am reading 'Faust' though," added Evelyn, laughing, as she rose, and thrust the book into a corner. "He has pronounced ideas about what women ought to read."

Again the movement and the words jarred Stella's candid and transparent soul, and again she got up uneasily, moving with the restlessness of one in a strange country, towards that sole familiar thing opposite her. This time, *seeing* the song on the desk, which she had only touched before, she said abruptly,

"Oh, you haven't sung!"

She had forgotten that Evelyn Marryot *could* sing.

"Will you sing me this?"

"If you wish it; but I am not fond of English songs, the words are for the most part so silly, and I dislike *songs without words*, except Mendelssohn's. Don't you? I think the 'sphere-born harmonious sisters, Voice and Verse,' were never meant to be sundered— voice exalted, verse neglected and slurred over. But what are you to make of this kind of thing?" said Evelyn, as she contemptuously

fingered the pages of her song, adding, with a
sort of dreamy mischief in her eyes :—

> " ' Wir reden und sehn,
>   Wir hören und reimen !
> *   *   *   *   *
>   Und wenn es uns glückt,
>   Und wenn es sich schickt,
>   So sind es Gedanken.' "

The quotation was a characteristic one, for
it was, naturally enough, the *clever* side of
" Faust " that had taken Evelyn Marryot's fancy
most—the brilliant Mephistophelean side ; and
it was the sparkling epigrams and flashes of
lambent satire that lingered in her memory.

Not that she was unfeeling. That sympathetic gentleness, that fine tact and tenderness
were not put on—only they did not go deep
enough. They seemed to have their origin in
the brain instead of in the heart, to pertain
rather to the intellectual and æsthetic than to
the emotional faculties.

And it was the same with her singing, Stella
thought that day. She could not tell whether
it was owing to her recent disenchantment, or
merely to the effect of greater nearness to the
singer ; but to day the voice that had chained
her so often, entranced, to the little balcony,
had no power to move her. The organ was

magnificent, the execution perfect; there were not wanting touches of pathos; the song itself was, from the musical point of view, interesting enough; and yet—there was something lacking; and Stella sat listening with only one feeling in her mind—thankfulness that the singing released her from talking.

She begged her cousin not to leave off, and Lady Marryot was looking for her third song, when she was interrupted by the arrival of a post. At the same time the servant handed her a note just delivered, he said, by Lord Holbrooke's skipper.

"But I should have got this sooner," she said, as she glanced over it. "He says the weather has altered so much for the better, he thinks it a pity not to have a cruise to-day, and hopes I will come on board at once; he will give me some lunch."

"Then I mustn't keep you," Stella said, cutting short all regrets and apologies with a better grace than she might have done, had she not been so relieved by the timely excuse for her projected departure.

Lady Marryot knew she would kindly excuse her glancing at a letter from Sir Henry, while she put on her wraps.

"Why, he's coming here to-morrow!" she

exclaimed the next minute. " Only fancy! I thought he was in Scotland, and he's at Carlisle, already on the way here! "

" I'm so glad for you," Stella said, receiving her cousin's parting embrace with considerable demureness.

She went back again to her motherly care-taker with a great sadness at her heart, yet with a sense of rest, as of one returning to a safe haven. She felt that she was happy to have in her daily companion a person who could not deceive, if she could not delight her, who would never waver in bestowing such good as she had to give, or ever rend her heart with disappointment.

Strange that there should be people to whom *happiness*—the wonderful word!—represents a negation merely! Tragically strange that there should exist—not a mood of mind, but a constant condition of mind in which the highest conceivable ideal of bliss is—suspension of torture!

But to-day that usually serene and cheerful face was clouded. The post had brought letters for Mrs. Thomson, too; one of them containing sad tidings of the children's invalid mother. Her disease had taken a fresh turn, and her sufferings were greatly augmented. She longed for her sister's return to the neighbourhood of St. Julyans, and the husband prayed that this might take place not later than the end of the week. His sister, who was now in charge, would be obliged to quit her post then.

"He is very good; he says he wouldn't but have me complete my three weeks here," said poor Mrs. Thomson, glancing ruefully at the babies who were beginning to look so bronzed and chubby, and doing such credit to her care. "But my poor Mary, I must get back to her—my poor Mary!"

Stella did not speak; but it was not on that account that Mrs. Thomson looked inquiringly into her face.

"One thing—it will be better for you than staying on," she said musingly. "The doctor has just been. He scolded me for letting you out. He said Devonsea was too cold for you—this strange season, at any rate. The other end of the town might have done——"

Mrs. Thomson paused. She was still taking that questioning survey. What more the doctor may have said she did not tell Stella.

The last days at Devonsea were uneventful enough. One afternoon Lady Marryot looked in to hope Stella was going on well. She talked music and poetry. She did not say a word about Sir Henry. She hesitated a little when Stella mentioned her approaching departure, then asked her to five o'clock tea the following day. Stella excused herself; she wished neither to meet her cousin against his will, nor to be markedly avoided by him.

Another afternoon, on the pier, she chanced to meet the whole family, face to face. She saw Sir Henry stop, and lean over the parapet to look at the sea or the sky, as his wife advanced towards her. Evelyn slipped her arm through hers and led her in the opposite direction, as though fondly imagining she had not noticed him among the people.

"Let us meet at Devonsea again," she said gently. "You are near, and I come often. I like the place. I shall long to hear of your music. Promise me that we shall meet again."

It was not possible to be hard upon this woman. There seemed, for all the mundane taint, to be a sort of longing in her—a longing genuine, if suppressed, after things true and lovely.

Something like pity for her shone in those calm, star-like eyes of Stella's, made calm by depth of purpose and by loftiness of aim. And it was sincerely that she thanked her for her goodness, as she called Guy to her, and hastened home.

VIII.

There is, perhaps, no music in the world—no solemn grandeur of organ, no caressing magic of violin—that goes to the heart like the music of a peal of church bells, mellowed by age, and hallowed by association.

Upon Stella's acutely sensitive organization, at any rate, the magnificent bells of the parish church at Astlett always had an effect quite distinct from that produced by any instrument. It was certainly not pain they gave her, but it was pleasure so keen as to become something strangely like it, so like it that she would often seek to avoid hearing them from very terror of their power over her. She would abstain from evening church on festival Sundays from dread of coming out into the awful star-light amid the deafening glory of the chimes, vibrating through and through her, and filling her with maddening longings, with that *Sehnsucht* that her German mother knew, and that is more than half despair. On practising days she would watch anxiously the direction of the wind, and long before the hour when the ringers began, would, if it was blowing from the church, betake her to the piano, or, if the piano were forbidden, to her closed and curtained room, where poring over "Charles Auchester" or Mendelssohn's Letters, with her head in her hands, she could hear but distant echoes of the siren sounds.

And think—if it was thus with her on common days—think what it was the day she heard them ringing the death-knell of love!

She had been back at Astlett three days—had come back just in time for the event she had gone joyfully to Devonsea in order to avoid.

It was a glorious September morning. The little town, Factory and all, was making holiday. More than one triumphal arch graced the road between the railway station and the future dwelling of the home-coming bride; flags and garlands fluttered from many a window in the High Street. A tincture of political feeling heightened the general excitement. There was a probability amounting to a certainty of a vacancy in the representation of Astlett; and the Liberal majority in the place already had their eye upon Gurney Head as a desirable, nay, an indispensable candidate. The remarkable degree of popularity he had won for himself among high and low was attested by the

merging of all class distinctions in the welcome
prepared for him. The tradespeople vied with
the Factory hands in doing him honour; the
young ladies whom he had enticed into joining
his Musical Society, notwithstanding its want of
selectness, socially speaking, had been foremost
in making arrangements with their humbler
confrères for a Wedding Hymn to be sung in
the garden.

The evening before, Kate Marshall had called
to say how glad they were to think they should
have Stella's contralto for a certain solo verse;
but Aunt Sarah had stepped in with a decided
negative that spared her the pain of answer-
ing. Stella's cough was far too bad to dream
of such a thing. If singing indoors was forbidden, what would the doctor say to standing
waiting about singing in the open air? So
Kate had gone home crestfallen, and Stella was
free to spend the morrow as she might.

It was sunny September, cool, but bright,
and the restlessness of misery drove her at midday from her chamber, where she had meant to
spend the day, out to her favourite post under
the willow, where she could smell the roses, and
watch the quiet river gliding by, and see, herself unseen, what little traffic there was upon
the road.

For the bridal carriage was not to pass that way.

And lo! all of a sudden, startling her out of her reverie, a merry peal, a hurrying clamour of joy-bells, borne straight to her on the fresh breeze, repeating its ecstatic outburst again and again, and again—

"Lest you should think [it] never could recapture
That first fine, careless rapture!"

There had been so much to think of—so much —she had forgotten the bells.

She could not flee them now.

She stood transfixed, with the tip of one of the lithe branches in her fingers, while the blood forsook her face, and her hands grew moist and cold.

For see, it was the death-knell of love! See, a woman must have love. Was she not made for it? Were not her eyes made to look unto the hand of a gentle master, her lips to seal soft baby-lips with kisses? Rob her of these joys, and give her what you will instead—admiration, success, fame itself—she will tell you— has told you—it is nothing but a "splendid mourning" for the other.

"Stella!" shouted a strident voice from the house. At the same time a heavy sash flew noisily upward. " Stella ! " repeated the voice impatiently, before the girl had time to answer.

" Yes, Aunt Catherine."

" Of course you are going to sing at the Cherry Orchard," began Miss Warren, through the folds of the knitted shawl she had thrown over her head and across her mouth.

Stella merely looked up at her inquiringly.

" I mean, you could get me my medicine this afternoon. Moss has sent the wrong medicine. Of course you'll sing ; won't you ? There'll be nothing to prevent that, I suppose, if you can stand about in the garden all the morning with nothing on."

" But I could go for your medicine now," put in Stella, scarcely knowing in her weary despair what she was saying.

" Well, the servants are busy, Elizabeth says ; but I wouldn't have anybody put themselves out. Your Aunt Sarah is out of the way. She always *is* out of the way when anything happens. Has she gone after this reception nonsense, do you think, or what ? It's pretty clear she's not in the house, or *you* wouldn't be where you are. Stella, do you hear what I say ? Don't look like an icicle ! *Do* tell me what I am to do, Stella ! "

" Oh, I'll go for it now," Stella said, as she

hurried into the house. And the sallow, sour face retreated from the window, and the sash thundered angrily down.

Stella was more than half glad to go. She knew that the town would be quiet enough in the morning; and as for the bells, they had stopped, and might not begin again till she had got home. It was better to be moving, moving briskly through the streets. She had gone out into the garden simply because it was better to be moving than to sit still. That is what all hunted creatures feel—it is better to be moving.

But what if she met acquaintance, and had to smile and to speak to them? There was little fear of that. People were reserving themselves for the afternoon; the volunteer choir would be practising; the townspeople trying to cram twelve hours' work into six. She set out bravely enough—in appearance, at least—to pace once more those familiar streets whose very familiarity had been used to stir and to inspire her. For "nothing is uniform to a soul really set on the idealities of art; everything, though it changes not, suggests to the mind of the musician."

There was one delightful red-brick house, genuine Queen Anne, in the High Street, now inhabited by a family of Heads, a house

that Stella always associated with some enchanting old-world air, some stately *"Menvet de
la Cour*," or sprightly *"Gavotte de Louis XV."*
To-day, as she passed it, with all fancy stricken
dead, all graceful imaginings frozen cold, somebody within chanced to be playing Roeckel's
"Air du Dauphin," and with a startled thrill she
paused to listen to the merry, airy music that
streamed gaily out through the open windows
into the quiet street. And as she lingered,
trembling and astonished at the contrasts of this
wonderful life, the fate that flings the rain upon
the harvest, and thrusts rejoicing upon stricken
hearts, the massive door flew open, and there
came out a flood of young life—Dolly and Kate
Marshall, the Harrison girls, and a detachment
of Heads, nieces and cousins of the bridegroom.

" Why, Stella, what are you doing here?
How's the cough? Aren't you going to sing?
I'm so sorry you can't sing," chorussed the
girls. " Going to Moss's? We are going
past Moss's—to the Cherry Orchard for a re-
hearsal. Such fun! and that dear old Mrs.
Head insists on our all lunching there."

So Stella was drawn into the vortex.

" Uncle Gurney *will* be disappointed at his
old friend not being there," said a kind little
Head girl, innocently.

"Oh, I hope we shall all see a great deal of him now," remarked a matter-of-fact cousin. "Stella certainly will, as soon as the Musical Society meets."

"Unless his wife cuts you out, Stella," laughed Dolly Marshall. "They say she has a contralto."

"Oh, there go those horrid bells again!" cried Kate from the rear. "I do hate those bells on week days."

"Why?"

"Oh, I don't know, it's so *Sundayish*. Of course I like Sunday, but *in its proper place*, don't you know?" At which brilliant sally the bevy joined in a ripple of girlish laughter.

In the midst of it Stella bade them good-bye, and slipped into the chemist's shop. Her errand there accomplished, she turned her steps homeward with a sense of prostration, bodily and mental, that came to her almost as a relief from the acuteness of her suffering. After all, there was a limit—a term even to that subtle agony which is inappreciable to the eyes of others, and eats away the solitary heart by imperceptible degrees; there was a bound where it was said unto secret pain, "*Hitherto* shalt thou come." Stella looked forward—not with a young girl's senti-

mental longing, but with a woman's strong
and deep desire—to the rest of death.

Her eyes were on the ground as she hurried
past the houses she knew. She did not see
that the solicitor's door was open, and that
there was a fly in front of it. She had got
well past it when she heard Mrs. Mahaffey's
cheery voice calling a farewell to her schoolboy
son. " Faith, and I won't forget it, my darling,
and don't *you* forget your old mother. Good-
bye, Phil, my darling! Good-bye, my blessing,
good-bye!"

" Why, Stella, how ill you look!" exclaimed
Aunt Sarah, in spite of herself, as she met
the girl in the hall.

" It isn't *my* fault!" screamed a voice from
the landing above. " *I* didn't send her out!
She was out already. I could have waited
for my medicine till next week. I could have
waited perfectly till next week for my medicine.
Stella, I hope you'll try and make your aunt
understand that you offered to go yourself.
I suppose you've not got it? Never mind.
I only thought some one would have brought
it up by this time."

" Miss Marryot's only just this moment come
in," panted the long-suffering Elizabeth, as
she flew upstairs with the parcel.

Miss Sarah stood quite still below examining Stella.

"Dear! How like your father you look!" she exclaimed, in spite of herself. "Now, do you *feel* worse this morning?"

"I don't feel very well to-day," Stella said.

"Ah, I thought you shouldn't have gone out to-day. I told Dr. Harrison so. We must ask him in again. Elizabeth, have the fire lit in Miss Marryot's room. Go up, dear, and just get between the sheets if you feel poorly. I shall see you again before dinner. You'll be better to-morrow."

"Elizabeth, do you think I'm very foolish to be here?" asked Stella of her faithful old friend, after she had crept into bed.

"I should think you very foolish if you was anywhere else," replied Elizabeth, with much decision. "You're not fit to be up."

She vouchsafed no further remark, but she did a good deal of gratuitous setting-to-rights in the room for "company," and as a safer outlet for sympathy than speech.

Stella's large eyes followed her.

"Elizabeth, what a kind person Mrs. Mahaffey seems!"

"So she do. That girl, Martha Wright, she often says what a kind mistress she was, and she wishes she'd never left her. There! Jane, if she lets that blind fly up that way we shall get it broke."

" Lizzie, do you remember when you used to call me 'darling?'"

" To be sure I do," said Elizabeth, pulling the blind up and down. " It would be funny if I didn't."

There were some remains of nursery cynicism about Elizabeth, for all her tender-heartedness, and she affected not to hear the sigh that came from Stella's bed—a long-drawn sobbing sigh, as of a tired child.

After that Stella left her bed very little.

The tenderest care and watching were hers. Sarah Warren seldom left her, and Elizabeth never. A physician of some repute from St. Julyans seconded Dr. Harrison's unwearying skill and kindness. The Astlett ladies—old Mrs. Head, Mrs. Mahaffey, the Marshall girls— came in and out with grapes and flowers.

One morning Mrs. Thomson hurried in with a letter in her hand.

She met Miss Sarah, looking very grave.

" I've brought something that will do her more good than fruit, though I wish I'd brought fruit," she said, holding up the letter. " This is about some songs my cousin has been trying to get published for her. She told you, I dare say?"

Sarah shook her head. "She's past that," she said, in a broken voice.

"So much worse?"

Sarah nodded.

And the other, kind soul, sat down to cry with her.

"Dr. Harrison says the *mind* must be kept perfectly quiet—as quiet as the house," Sarah said, after a while. "Nothing to excite her."

"Ah, everything to do with music always did excite her so curiously," said Mrs. Thomson. "I'm sorry. I had hoped it would be a little pleasure for her."

"Would they take her songs?"

"Take them? Not only take them, but they're prepared to give a good sum for them, my cousin says. They always try to get them for nothing at first, she says; but, you see, she's an old hand, and she seems to have made a good bargain for Stella. Poor Stella!"

"Only think!" exclaimed Miss Sarah. "Think of her having so much talent!"

"Yes, indeed. Listen. 'There is no question about their being excellent compositions—indeed they are almost *too good* to be *popular*. Still, one, at any rate, is so charming in point of melody, besides being almost faultless in construction, that, for my own part, I have little doubt of its launching your friend into well-deserved popularity—a thing we composers can't afford to despise. Do tell me more about her age, history, etc. Of course these are not first attempts. Is she as poor as I am? I must know this genius of yours.' "

" *Genius!* Only think!" echoed Miss Sarah, whom the notion bewildered a little. " Poor Stella! poor child! She *would* have been pleased. I wonder now if Dr. Harrison would give leave—if it would be possible—— "

" Oh, *do* let us," pleaded Mrs. Thomson. " You can't think how curiously she seemed to care about everything to do with music at Devonsea ; it was most singular."

" There's the doctor now ; I'll ask him," interrupted Miss Sarah, as she hurried into the passage.

Mrs. Thomson sat listening to the whispered colloquy.

" Oh dear, yes ; anything of *that* kind," she heard Dr. Harrison say. " Oh, that would be a little amusement for her. I merely meant anything at all agitating."

But while he was speaking, Elizabeth came running down the stairs with a face as white

as death. " I believe she's gone in her sleep,"
she said.

There was nobody in' Astlett that was not
shocked and startled to hear of Stella's death.
It had been such a familiar little face; the
illness had been so short; she had seemed so
healthy until comparatively lately. Still they
all knew that there was consumption in her
father's family, and the medical verdict that
death had resulted from an insidious form of
the hereditary disease had been, of course, un-
hesitating.

At first—that is to say.

For a time came—a long while afterwards—
when Dr. Harrison was heard to make the
casual observation that Stella Marryot's. case
had puzzled him a little; that certain of the
symptoms had pointed in a curious manner to
what, in any one else, he should certainly have
called mental distress; that the rapidity of the
fatal termination had not been altogether satisfactorily accounted for; and that, *but for her
never having had any trouble*, he should have
said she had died of a broken heart.

THE END.

LONDON : PRINTED BY WILLIAM CLOWES AND SONS, LIMITED,
STAMFORD STREET AND CHARING CROSS.

www.ingramcontent.com/pod-product-compliance
Lightning Source LLC
Chambersburg PA
CBHW021842070726
47496CB00022B/1823